Exiled!

Fron Tragedy to Triumph
on the Missouri Frontier

LOUISE A. JACKSON

EAKIN PRESS ⱽⱽ Fort Worth, Texas
www.EakinPress.com

Dedication

This book is in honor of the generations of women in my family named Ruth: *Ruthy Leeper*, who moved with her children from Tennessee to Missouri in 1833, to begin again after her husband died; *Ruth Ann Leeper Cawlfield,* who became a pioneer wife in the new state of Texas; *Ruth Harriet Cawlfield Darter,* who endured the Civil War, caught between a father and brothers who "went for the Union" and a husband who did not; and their descendants, especially *Ruth Madeline Darter Kennedy Robison, Ruth Ottilie Darter McMaster*, and *Connie Ruth Darter Cox.*

Contents

A Note from the Author

While writing about the adventures of Ephraim Darter in a previous novel, *Gone To Texas: From Virginia to Adventure*, I frequently reminded myself that travel in the nineteenth century would be very different for a girl. It was partly to satisfy my curiosity about how those differences might play themselves out that I decided to write *Exiled!*

I borrowed the names of my great-great-grandmother, Ruth Ann Leeper and her mother, Ruthy, both of whom did indeed travel from Hawkins County, Tennessee, to Greene County, Missouri, in the early part of the 19th century. That much is fact. All the rest of the story is based on careful research, including a trip along Ruthy's route that was as nearly the same as existing roads and ferries would allow, and my own imagination.

The year in which the book is set, 1837, coincides with the beginning of the first Great Depression in the United States. It was called the "Panic of 1837." Widespread crop failures in both 1836 and 1837 added to the hardships caused by the closing of banks and the general hard times.

This period in our history was also a time of great religious fervor in the United States. It was called "The Second Great Awakening." The religious emphasis in Ruthy's family is quite typical of the movement's results in the Appalachian regions of Kentucky and Tennessee.

Ruthy's *Housewife Book* is modeled on an actual one. Recipes, remedies, and household hints were always entered in the order in which they were learned.

My research highlighted the sturdy determination that led our ancestors to leave their established homes and start all over again in new places, farther west. I salute them all.

—LOUISE A. JACKSON
Springfield, Missouri

P.S. Please note the glossary in the back. It can be a big help.

Acknowledgments

Any writer of historical fiction always owes debts of gratitude to helpful reference librarians and I am no exception. Without these dedicated professionals, research would be much more difficult and certainly less productive. In particular, I extend a heartfelt thank-you to the many wonderful people from the following:

Springfield/Greene County Library, Springfield, Missouri; Meyer Library, Missouri State University; Springfield/Greene County History Museum; Western Historical Manuscript Collection, University of Missouri-Columbia; The Library of Congress: American Memory Team & Geography and Map Division, Washington, D.C.; and, especially, to all the dedicated staffs of the many public libraries in Tennessee, Kentucky, Illinois, and Missouri who dropped what they were doing to help a weary traveler on a tight schedule, most particularly the Hawkins County

Branch of the Nolichucky Regional Library in Rogersville, Tennessee.

I am also grateful beyond measure to the following: Virginia Messer and the rest of the Eakin Press family, all of whom work to make my books look good, as well as my friend and mentor, Barbara Clayton, and the members of the Springfield Writers Workshop. Each of them gave me careful critiques and useful suggestions.

Finally, many thanks to my husband, Don, for his suggestions, his forbearance, and his help, particularly during our research trip as we followed Ruthy's route from Rogersville, Tennessee, to Springfield, Missouri.

Exiled!

LOUISE A. JACKSON

Ruth Ann Donohue: Her Journal

A gift from her mother,

Christmas, 1836

Wed. June 9, 1837
Hawkins County, Tenn.

I can't go to sleep tonight. It's important to look rested, they told me. But I won't be. Tomorrow keeps tumbling around in my head. Papa says it will be all right, but what if it isn't? What if it all goes against me? Not knowing what to expect is the hardest part of all.

From this day, forward, I am resolved to control my temper, even if I do have red hair.

CHAPTER 1

Verdict

Two hours after they left to consider the case, the Hawkins County, Tennessee, jury, Court Session, Summer, 1837, straggled back into the courtroom. It was stifling hot inside, even with all the tall glass windows raised as far as they would go.

Twelve-year-old Ruthy Donohue watched closely. She knew nearly every man in the line. Except for a few who lived over beyond Surgoinsville, most were neighbors and friends of her family. Still, right then, they all looked like complete strangers. Nothing about them looked familiar. She reached for her father's hand.

One ... two ... three ... four ... She counted the jurors as they came into the jury box. ... Nine ... ten ... eleven ... Why did they move so slow? The last chair still stood empty. The court waited. The judge frowned. Finally, Mr. Congers, the last juror, came through the door, adjusting his trousers,

5

and the twelve men sat down. Whispers rose from the crowded courtroom. Ruthy even heard a couple of giggles.

Judge McIntosh glared at the audience and rapped his gavel on the table where he sat. "Court will be in order." The room hushed. Some of the women in the room even stopped waving their fans. He turned to the twelve men. "In the case of Jeremiah McMinn's family vs. Ruth Ann Donohue, have you reached a verdict?"

Mr. Hamilton stood. "I reckon we have, yer honor."

"What is your decision?"

This was it. Ruthy leaned against her father's shoulder, gripped his hand tighter and swallowed hard. Her heart felt as if it would jump out of her chest. All the rest of her life depended on Mr. Hamilton's next words.

Behind her, sitting in the first row, her mother whispered, "Hold your head up, child. Sit tall."

The jury foreman shifted from one foot to the other. He cleared his throat. "Well . . . ," He cleared his throat and started again. "Well, we think she shot him, Judge. But we're purty sure it was an accident, just like she and her pa said. The truth is, a man shouldn't leave his rifle leaning up against the doorframe like he did. Especially with it half-cocked."

He turned and looked at Ruthy's father, dressed in his Sunday-best black wool suit and white shirt, and then at Ruthy, in her new green print dress, as they sat in front of the judge's table. "Most of us have knowed this little girl all her life. She's got a temper to go with that hair, but she ain't no killer. It had to be an accident."

Ruthy felt her father's shoulders sag. Tears of relief

sprang to her eyes. A loud buzz ran through the crowd like a hot summer wind through the trees. Many heads nodded. Several angry murmurs rumbled. Someone in the back cried out, "No, that ain't right!" Up close, Ruthy heard her mother's soft "Thank you, Lord!"

Judge McIntosh acted quickly. Crash! He pounded his gavel on the table in front of him. Crash! Crash! "Order," he roared. "Order in the courtroom. Order, I say!"

Quiet slowly returned.

The judge looked at the other eleven men. "Do you all agree?" The rest of the jurors nodded.

"So be it. Will the defendant rise?"

Ruthy stood. Her father stood with her. He put his hand on her shoulder.

"Ruth Ann Donohue," the judge pronounced, "the jury says it was an accident and, according to the law, that's that. Still, a boy from our community, one we all knew, is dead because you picked up a gun when you shouldn't have."

The judge paused, scanned the audience, and seemed to consider his next words carefully. "This court has heard the jury, but is also aware of the bereaved family and its feelings. As a tribute to Jeremiah, then, this court sentences you to the following. You must stand before the dead boy's family and express your sincere regrets. You can't leave your pa's place for one month except to go to church on Sundays. Finally, you must appear before me at the next court session, three months from now, and give a full account of your behavior and actions from now until then." He paused and looked at Ruthy, obviously expecting a response.

In a small voice, Ruthy said, "Yes, Sir—I mean, Your Honor. I will. I'll do it all."

"As for you, William Donohue," Judge McIntosh continued, "this court is also mindful of your careless handling of your firearm. You are hereby admonished."

Ruthy's father bowed his head, sorrow and regret written in every line of his face.

"Well, then, you can all go home." The gavel sounded one last time. "Court's adjourned."

RITHY'S JOURNAL

Thursday, Sept. 10, 1837

Papa was right. Things did come out all right. But the judge was right, too. The gun fired when I picked it up and Jeremiah is dead. I will never forget that awful day, no matter how long I live. I don't think I can ever bear to touch a gun again. I shall try my best to hold onto my temper, even if someone does tease me till I can't bear it, then jerks my chair out and dumps me on the floor.

CHAPTER 2

Restricted

Judge McIntosh's sentence became truly real to Ruthy two days later, when she had to stay home instead of going back to Rogersville, the county seat and nearest town.

"Will you bring me something?" Ruthy asked, looking up to where her parents sat on the wagon. "Some candy or something?"

"Maybe so," Mama said.

"Maybe not," Papa said. "Candy can wait until this month is over."

"But, William ...," Mama opened her mouth to protest.

Papa took both reins in one hand and laid the other hand on Mama's knee. She closed her mouth in a straight line and looked at her shoes.

"We'll be home before dark," Papa said.

"You could work on your sampler," Mama said. "Or the pinwheel blocks for your quilt. I left warm water by the fire.

9

Be sure to get your bath so you'll be ready for church tomorrow."

Wanting to delay the moment when she would be alone, Ruthy asked, "Will you eat at the inn? Will you bring me some of your dinner?"

"I'm taking food with us," Mama said. "The inn is for special days. This is just a trip to town."

"That's enough talking, you two," Papa said. "We need to get going." He released the wagon brake and slapped the reins across the horses' backs. "Get up, there."

Buck and Betsy moved forward; the wagon rolled away. Ruthy watched them out of sight, with her hand held up halfway to her shoulder. If her folks waved, she'd be ready to wave back. But Papa had his arm across Mama's back and neither one waved.

Ruthy took her bath first thing after they left, so the water wouldn't get cold. It was nice to be the first to use the bath water. Usually, she hopped in the wooden washtub after Mama got out. Papa was good about that. Better than most men, Mama said. He always dumped his own bath water on the rose bush by the porch and brought in clean water for her and Mama.

"We're spoiled," Mama said. "But don't tell your father I said so."

After her bath, Ruthy embroidered one letter on her sampler, then smoothed the cloth with her hand and sighed. She should have finished this by now. Her friend Josie's sampler was already framed and hanging on the wall at her house. But it was so hard to sit and make all those little even stitches. Still, she didn't want people to think Mama hadn't brought her up proper. She started again. She could at least finish this line. It said, *"Learning is a beauty bright ..."*

She stopped three times before putting the last stitch in the "t." Once she thought she heard a hawk scream and went outside to check the chickens. Awhile later, she stopped to go to the outhouse. The last time, she peered through the front window to see what Molly, the family dog, was barking at. Whatever it was must have run away. Ruthy couldn't see anything. She sighed again, even louder than before, and went back to that dratted sampler.

The sun was as high as it was going to get when she finished. Ruthy crammed the embroidered cloth into her sewing box, flexed her fingers and stretched.

Cold biscuit and ham along with a cup of buttermilk from the springhouse made a good lunch, but it was over too soon. It was so quiet Ruthy could hear the house creak and the hens cluck. Mama and Papa probably wouldn't be back for hours. What should she do next? Not the quilt blocks. She'd done enough needlework for one day. Maybe she ought to tug the washtub to the door and dump it outside. No, too heavy for one.

She wandered through the whole downstairs—the big kitchen, the dogtrot down the middle, and the front room Mama called the parlor. Ruthy straightened Grandfather Malloy's portrait as she walked by it in the front room. Then she went upstairs to the two bedrooms. One was for her parents. The other used to be shared by her brothers while she slept in a trundle bed in her parents' room. Then, when both boys grew up and moved out, she got the second bedroom all to herself.

After her tour, she went outside and poked around the yard. The last rose on the bush by the front steps drooped. When she touched it, the petals fluttered to the ground. Molly, their black and white hound, came from somewhere and thrust her nose into Ruthy's hand, receiving a brief pat. Finally, she sat on the porch for awhile and looked across the fields to the long line of hills holding their small valley close.

Back inside, Ruthy thought about starting supper. But she didn't do that either. Twenty-nine more days of restriction. It didn't bear thinking about. Completely discouraged, she dragged into the parlor and looked at the books on the table by her father's chair. The Holy Bible, the *Complete Works of Shakespeare*, and *The Sketch Book* by Washington Irving. She thought about reading Rip Van Winkle again but chose Shakespeare instead and was nearly at the end of trying to puzzle out *Macbeth* when Molly's welcoming bark signaled an end to her long day.

"At least I got something done on my sampler," she thought as she hurried to the door. "Mama will be glad about that."

Saturday night:

   Today was quite long. I had to stay home by myself. Molly-dog was luckier than me I. She found something to interest her, even if I didn't. She barked and barked. Tomorrow is church. I shall wear my dress with the blue flowers and puffed sleeves.
   I hope Josie is at church. I miss her.

CHAPTER 3

Shunned

Next morning, Papa pulled the wagon to a stop in front of the small, unpainted, frame church. The building had two front doors—one for the men and boys and one for the women and girls. Several families clustered outside in small groups, talking and enjoying the fresh air before church began.

"Looks like we're going to have a good crowd this morning," Mama commented.

Ruthy hopped to the ground. Mama followed, stepping carefully.

"I won't be long," Papa said. "It'll only take a minute to tie up."

"Take your time," Mama answered. "I want to ask Emmeline if I can walk over next week and borrow her *Godey's Lady's Book*."

Ruthy looked for Josie, first thing. Maybe they could sit

together. She spotted her friend easily, standing next to her mother. Mrs. Todd was a tall woman with a long, thin face.

"Josie," Ruthy called. She waved and hurried toward the Todds.

Josie's face lighted up. She stepped forward quickly, only to be yanked back, turned around, and propelled abruptly toward the women's door by Mrs. Todd's strong grip.

Ruthy hesitated. She was sure Josie had seen her. Mrs. Todd had, too. What was their hurry? Church hadn't started yet. There wasn't any bell to ring. Brother Kelvin always came to the door when it was time to go in.

Josie looked back with an apology on her face just before disappearing into the building.

Puzzled, Ruthy walked back to her mother's side in time to hear something else out of the ordinary. Mrs. Emmeline Boykin, who lived on the place next to theirs, was refusing to lend her pattern book. "I'm sorry, Martha. I can't. Maybe later." She glanced at the other women, most of whom had turned their backs. In a softer voice, she added, "You know how it is. Give things some time."

Mama stared at her neighbor. "I see. Thank you, Emmeline. I understand all too well. Come, Ruthy. Your father is waiting."

On the way home after church, Mama poured out all her hurt and frustration. "The nerve of those women," she sputtered. "There they sat, never looking at us, pretending to be God-fearing people and not showing the least bit of charity. Not even a smidgen! Not even a dab!"

Ruthy slumped against her mother, misery in every line of her body. "It's all my fault."

Mama gathered Ruthy close. "Nonsense," she said. "It's the fault of those judgmental people. 'Judge not, lest ye be judged,' I say. What if the shoe was on the other foot? Then see what they'd think!" She turned to Papa. "William, was it the same on the men's side? I couldn't tell, from where we sat."

Papa flicked the reins. "Well, put it this way, the other men didn't go out of their way to say much. But then, a lot of them never do. Still, I'm sure they noticed that Brother Kelvin's text was *Vengeance is mine, saith the Lord.*" He patted Mama's knee. "I think Emmeline was right. Give it some time. Something else will soon come along for you ladies to gossip about and it will all blow away."

He mulled the situation over for a few more turns of the wagon wheels, then squinched up his eyes and sniffed loudly. "You know, I can tell we're nearly home, even with my eyes shut. Don't I remember seeing some fried chicken before we left? I'm sure I can smell it." He flicked the reins again. "Get up, there, Buck. Move along, Betsy. I'm a hungry man!"

Sunday night

How can people be so mean? I don't think Josie intended it. Her mama made her walk away. I'm pretty sure about that. All the grownups hate us. And it's all because of me. If only I could go back and do that awful day over again!

CHAPTER 4

Hard Labor

Monday dawned bright and clear. At breakfast, Mama declared it was time to wash clothes. "Hard work keeps minds free from worry," she said.

"I'll get the fire started and fill the washpot before I go to the field," Papa told her.

Mama gathered and sorted clothes. Ruthy didn't have to be told what her part was. She knew. She had to fill those heavy old washtubs with water. When Aaron and Jesse were still home, that had been their job. Now, though, with her brothers grown and gone, Ruthy had to do it all.

The tubs were made of wooden staves held together with iron bands. Ruthy strained to lift them from their pegs on the back wall of the house. She put two of them side by side on a rough bench and the other on the ground near the washpot.

Bucket by bucket, back and forth, she carried water

from the spring. By the time the tubs were full, Ruthy's arms ached and the sides of her skirt were dripping wet from where the water sloshed out as she walked.

All morning long, Mama and Ruthy did the washing. "White things first," Mama said. She shaved slivers of lye soap and dropped them into the boiling water. "Then the colors."

Papa's greasy, dirty overalls and the scrub rags went last.

First, they soaked the clothes in the tub of cold water near the fire. That got the easy dirt out so the hot water stayed a bit cleaner. Next, the two wrung the water from the soaked clothes and put them in the pot. Ruthy kept the fire going while Mama punched the garments up and down in the boiling, soapy water. Boiling helped melt the sweat and body oils out of the cloth.

"I guess that's long enough," Mama said. She lifted each steaming piece from the pot with a long, smooth stick and dropped it in the water bucket. Once a piece slipped off the end of the stick and fell into the dirt. Drat! It had to go back in the soaking tub and start all over again.

Ruthy took the hot clothes to the washbench and dumped them in the left-hand tub, the one with the washboard standing in it. She sighed to think of all the work still to do. Spread a garment on the board. Rub the bar of soap over it. Turn the cloth over and scrub it up and down, up and down, over the ridges in the board. Try not to scrape your knuckles. Wring out the soapy water. Drop the piece into the rinse water to the right. Pick up the next piece.

Dip the newly washed clothes up and down, up and

down, in the rinse water. Wring the clothes out again and hang them to dry on a fence or spread them on some bushes.

It took a lot of running back and forth to keep everything going at once.

"Hurry, Ruthy, I need that bucket again."

"The fire's getting low, Ruthy. We need more wood."

"Ruthy, if you don't get over here and catch the other ends of these sheets, we'll never get through."

"Be careful, child! Don't burn your skirt." It was a good thing they only wore one petticoat on washday. The closer your skirt hung to your limbs, the safer you were.

"There," Mama sighed. "That's the last piece! Let's put the fire out and go in. I look for Papa to be here any minute, starving to death, like always."

No wonder they ate cold food at noon on washday, Ruthy thought. There wasn't any time to cook. Plus, they were too hot and tired to do another single thing.

After Papa ate, he went back to the field. Mama used some of the soapy wash water to scrub the porch. Ruthy filled a pail with the second rinse water and poured it on the flowers by the front porch. She re-hung the tubs, bucket, and washboard on their pegs. When the clothes were dry, she brought them in.

During supper, Ruthy poked at her food. Keeping her eyes on her plate, she said, "The hard work didn't do its job. I'm still thinking about what the judge said—about me saying 'I'm sorry' to Jeremiah's family." She looked up. "What if they don't want to see me? What if they slam the door in my face?" Her imagination raced. "What if they won't open the door at all? What if they throw eggs at me?" She shuddered.

"Ruthy Donohue, stop that nonsense right now!" Mama scolded. "Don't look for trouble before it comes looking for you. Remember what the Scripture says. *Sufficient unto the day is the evil thereof.*"

"If that's the case, I'd better wait awhile" Ruthy said. "To go to see them, I mean. I don't need any more evil right now.

"Waiting only makes things worse," Papa said. "I'll tell you what—I'll go to town in the next day or two and see what Sheriff Tate suggests. Maybe if he went out there first and sort of paved the way, told them we were coming, it might make things easier. He's good about doing things like that. He'll know how to handle it.

"Settle down, now, and finish your food."

RUTHY'S JOURNAL

Monday night

I'm too tired to write much tonight. Besides, I don't have anything to say. Except I wish my hands didn't get so red and wrinkled on wash-day. And I really wish I didn't have to go see Jeremiah's family. What can I tell them that I haven't already said?

CHAPTER 5

Threatened

"Papa, I'm scairt." Ruthy smoothed her skirt and carefully traced her finger around the outline of a blue flower on the fabric of her Sunday dress.

A week and a day had passed since the court handed down its verdict. The Donohue family was on its way to Jeremiah's house.

"You don't need to be," Papa said. "They know we're coming. They told the sheriff they'd look for us today." He eased the wagon wheels over a chug-hole in the road. "Remember, Ruthy, our two families have always been close. Henry and I well nigh grew up together. The McMinns won't forget that even after all that's happened."

Mama wrapped her arm around Ruthy's shoulders and squeezed.

"Tell me again what the sheriff said," Ruthy asked.

"He rode out to the McMinn place, and talked to Henry

and Naomi. They said you could speak your piece and they'd listen." Papa guided Buck and Betsy off the main road and onto a winding, rutted lane. "Are you sure in your own mind what you're going to say?"

"I thought I was, when we started out. I've practiced it over and over. You heard me. But ... what if I forget? What if all the words go right out of my head?"

Mama chuckled and elbowed Ruthy's ribs. "If they fly out, I'll catch them and put them right back inside. I'll stick 'em in through here." She poked her finger gently into her daughter's ear. "That will take care of any runaway words!"

Her voice grew serious. "Say a little prayer, child, and breathe deep. You're a Donohue. Donohues are strong people. You can do this."

"Here we are," Papa said. He stopped the wagon, wrapped the reins around the brake lever and stepped down. Walking to the other side, he held out his hands to his daughter. "It's time."

Ruthy let Papa help her down and looked toward the old, familiar log house with the tulip poplar tree just outside the door. The rope swing she and Jeremiah used to play on hung from one strong limb. Leaves filled the hollow their feet had worn beneath it.

Mama was still in the wagon when the front door opened and a whole string of people came out and lined up, shoulder to shoulder. Ruthy had known them all, ever since she could remember: Jeremiah's father, mother, two older brothers, their wives, Jeremiah's two sisters, and his granny. They stood in complete silence, waiting. Mrs. McMinn's folded arms hugged her chest tightly. Granny's sharp black eyes glared from under the brim of her poke bonnet.

Ruthy slowly planted one foot in front of the other and moved forward. A flop-eared hound ambled over and nosed her skirt. Stopping, she patted his head. He licked her hand and started to jump up.

Mr. McMinn's sharp command cut through the air. "Git away, thar!" The dog tucked his tail and moved back.

Ruthy looked at the two she called "Mr. Henry and Miz Naomi." She opened her mouth. Nothing came out. She swallowed and tried again. Still nothing. Tears flooded her eyes. She reached out her hand as if begging for help.

"What's the matter, Miss Redhead?" Granny McMinn's high, cracked voice taunted. "Guilt got your tongue?"

Ruthy's hand dropped. She looked in the direction of the taunt. "No, I ..."

"Ma," Mr. Henry cautioned.

"Don't 'Ma' me, Henry McMinn," Granny said. "I aim to have my say. This girl that I rocked on my own lap when she was little, has turned out wrong, and if nobody else will say it, I will. That temper of hern is the Devil's own and if she don't suffer for it now, it will get her in the end."

She turned back to Ruthy. "You listen to me, young lady. Go home and pray to be delivered. Then, someday when you've learned the kind of suffering you've put this family through, come back. Maybe then you'll deserve forgiveness."

Granny's words hit like heavy hammer blows. Ruthy staggered back under the impact, only to be stopped by Papa's solid body, standing just behind. She drew in her breath. It was all so unfair. Ruthy was as sorry as she could be about Jeremiah. She'd said so, over and over. She knew no apology was ever going to be enough. But what else could she do?

She'd never meant it to happen. Never! All she aimed to do was aggravate Jeremiah just like he'd been aggravating her. She wasn't about to let him pull a chair out from under her and dump her on the floor and get away with it. But he ran into the yard and out of her reach.

"Next time you do that, Jeremiah McMinn," she'd yelled from the door, "I'll ... I'll ..." She'd looked around for the worst threat she could think of. "I'll shoot you that's what! With this very gun." And she'd picked up Papa's rifle, leaning right there against the doorframe. It was lots heavier than she expected, and longer too. She'd heaved the barrel up and waved it in the general direction of the laughing boy.

Then there was a bang and Jeremiah was down and ...

Ruthy swallowed hard and shook her head. It just happened, that's all. And, if she tried for the rest of her life, she couldn't make it go away. Why wouldn't they understand that?

"Well, missy?" Granny said.

An uninvited heat rose up from somewhere in Ruthy's chest and flooded her face. A strange buzzing invaded her head. Her tears dried. Granny McMinn was a mean, spiteful old woman! Always had been. Everybody said so. Even her lap bones poked and prodded, Ruthy remembered.

The carefully prepared speech vanished. Ruthy clenched her fists. Her mouth flew open as if it had a mind of its own and the girl who had come to apologize blurted out the first thing that came into her head.

"I'm not, either, bad!" Ruthy said. She glared at Granny McMinn. "Mr. Henry and Miz Naomi know I'm not, and you oughtn't to say things like that. They just aren't true. I *am* sorry! I am!"

Ignoring the tears flowing down her cheeks, she continued. "I'm going to pray, all right. But not for me. For *you*! For you to be delivered from ... from ... from meanness, that's what."

To Ruthy's complete disgust, her last words, intended to be brave, came out as a hiccup. Turning, she fled to the wagon, leaned against the wheel and sobbed until her throat was raw.

The grownups, except for Granny, stood awkwardly silent, as if unsure of what should happen next. The old woman never hesitated. She wheeled around, skirts flying, and stalked back to the cabin. Moments later, the rest of the family straggled after her. All but Mr. Henry. He came over and said a quiet word to Papa, his long-time friend. Papa said something back, returned to the wagon and the Donohues drove away.

As soon as they were out of earshot, Mama asked, "What did Henry say, back there at the end? I couldn't hear from where I was at." Her hands kept busy, rubbing Ruthy's back and wiping the tears from her damp cheeks.

"Ahh, he said Ruthy didn't need to say any more and he apologized for Granny. Said she was old and seemed like she got crankier every day she lived. Which," Papa added, "he didn't have to tell us none. We've knowed that for years."

"That's the almighty truth," Mama said.

"He's going to talk to her—said she'd prob'ly come around in time. I'm not too sure of that, but I figure time's all we got. Not much else to do but wait it out. Think how we'd feel if the shoe was on the other foot. "

Mama nodded. "I have. But Henry's right. Time heals most wounds." She considered her words for several heart-beats, then added, "But not all."

The Donohues rode the rest of the way home in silence as Buck and Betsy followed the bumpy road, up hill and down, over and around.

Ruthy listened to her parents in despair. She'd done it again! Flown off the handle and caused trouble. Seemed like she wasn't ever going to learn. Why couldn't she have had brown hair? Or whitish? Anything but red! Everybody said red hair and hot temper went together, and it must be true. Look at her.

The shadows were lengthening by the time the family neared home. As Papa swung the wagon toward the barn, Mama dug her fingers into his arm.

"Stop, William. Something's wrong." She peered toward the front porch.

Papa pulled back on the reins. "Whoa, now. Whoa. What is it?" he asked.

"I can't quite tell," Mama said. She squinted her eyes. "It looks like something's hanging from the roof. Whatever it is, it wasn't there when we left."

"I'll go see," Ruthy said. She half-stood, but Mama grabbed her skirt and pulled her back.

Papa set the brake and stepped down, whistling for

Molly. Molly didn't come. He whistled again. Still nothing. "That dog never is around when I need her," he grumbled. "She shows up fast enough when it's feeding time." He moved toward the porch.

Ruthy couldn't stand it another minute. She twitched her skirt from Mama's grasp and sprang down, determined to see, for herself, whatever it was. Edging up behind her father, she peeked around him. "It's a doll of some sort," she said.

They walked closer.

"No doll," Papa said. He took another step and stopped again. "Ruthy," he said quietly, without looking around. "Go back to the wagon." His deliberate voice gave no room for backtalk. "Now!"

Ruthy went. From the wagon she and her mother watched as Papa slipped through the shadows until he'd gone all the way around the house.

"What was it, Ruthy?" Mama wanted to know.

"Some sort of doll, I think, made out of rags. I didn't see anything else."

Papa came back and, ignoring Mama's urgent questions, led Buck and Betsey to the barn. Inside, he looked around again and called softly, "Molly! Here, girl." But Molly wasn't in the barn either.

Leaving his team standing in their harnesses, Papa picked up a pitchfork and extended a hand to help Mama down. "I believe we'll go in the back way. Stay close."

28

Inside the house, with the back door barred, Papa leaned his pitchfork against the wall and walked across the room, toward the front.

"Shall I light a candle?" Mama asked. It was nearly dark inside the house.

"Not yet. I need my evening eyes right now." Papa lifted his rifle from the pegs above the door and checked the priming. "Now we'll see what we can see," he said, as he reached for the front door latch.

Mama clutched Ruthy to her side. "Oh, be careful!" she begged. Her eyes followed every move Papa made.

Papa stepped onto the front porch and looked both ways. He listened carefully and whistled a third time for Molly. "Dratted dog," he muttered. He untied the doll-like thing hanging from the eave of the porch and examined it carefully. Finally, he came back inside and leaned the rifle against the wall. Catching himself, he picked the gun up and returned it once more to the pegs above the door.

Ruthy slipped from under her mama's clutching arm. "What is it, Papa? Let me see."

Mama hurried to stir up the fire and light a candle.

Papa tossed a roughly-crafted rag doll onto the table. His laugh sounded forced and awkward. "It's just a piece of meanness. Probably somebody who didn't have enough to do at home. Nothing to worry about."

Mama held the candle high. She gasped and covered her mouth with her free hand.

The doll was about as long as Ruthy's arm and carelessly put together. It looked as if someone had stuffed one end of a bag with straw and tied a hangman's noose just under the stuffing to make a head. The rest of the bag hung loosely, like a skirt. Rough eyes and a mouth, already smeared from handling, were drawn with charcoal. A long, sharp thorn pinned on the yarn used for hair.

Ruthy couldn't take her eyes from that hair. It hung loose and was dyed red. Now she understood Mama's fearful gasp. The doll was meant to be her.

RUTHY'S JOURNAL

Friday night

That awful doll! I shudder to think about it. Papa made out like he thought it was just meanness and nothing would come of it, but Mama and I think Papa is as worried as we are. I wonder where Molly is. She still hasn't come up. Oh, I wish Josie were here right now so I could talk with her.

"That's all we can do for you, old girl. It's up to you, what happens next."

They laid Molly near the chimney, on a worn quilt. Ruthy set a dish of water nearby and replaced the cool compress. The first one was already hot. It seemed like such a little thing to do—to put a wet rag on the hurt place. She wondered if the herb-woman who came that time when she had measles knew how to help dogs, too. It would sure be handy to know what to do when someone was sick or hurt. At least Papa knew how to put Molly's leg back together.

"I wish I knew how to fix things, Molly," Ruthy said. She sat down on the floor and watched the dog's chest go up and down with each breath. "Maybe, someday, I can learn how to do more."

RUTHY'S JOURNAL

Saturday night

Tomorrow is church day. Papa says the ox is in the ditch like the Good Book says and we need to stay home so we can take care of Molly and watch over the place. Mama says if we stay home, all those snooty people will win. I can't decide. The judge said I had to go, but he doesn't know about the hangman's doll. That changes things. It would be nice to see Josie, though. I wonder what we'll do.

CHAPTER 7

Decision

Papa had his way. They stayed home. But Mama and the judge had their way too. Ruthy didn't miss church. After breakfast, Mama brought the big family Bible to the table and Papa read a chapter. Then, because Mama said Ruthy needed the practice, Ruthy read a chapter too. Some of the words were hard and she stumbled a bit but she got through it. That done, they sang a church song and Papa said, "Amen."

As soon as he said, "Amen," he shoved his chair back and stood, reaching for his hat. "I believe I'll show my face outside for a bit," he said. "If someone is watching, they'll find out right away that we're here."

"What about Molly?" Ruthy asked, looking toward the chimney corner. "Did you notice she can stand up, now?"

Molly heard her name and thumped her tail against the wall.

"Yes," Papa said. "She's still shaky but, when I took her out before breakfast, she did well enough."

"Good," Mama said with relief. "Then get her out of my kitchen."

Papa grinned, whistled, and slapped his leg. "Let's go, Molly. We can tell when we're not wanted."

Molly slowly unfolded her legs and stood, the splinted leg angled outward. She swayed slightly and cocked her head to see better out of her good eye.

Papa made a sucking sound with his lips and slapped his leg again. "Come on, girl."

Molly staggered from her corner and followed. Her splint tip-tapped as she limped across the floor, but as soon as her feet hit the back porch, she lay down again and curled up, content to stay where she was.

The hours passed slowly. Other than church and visiting, there wasn't a lot to do on Sunday. It was supposed to be a day of rest. Taking care of people and animals was all right, but regular work was wrong. Mama walked some with Papa while he made his rounds. She laid out a cold lunch, cleared the dishes, read some in the Bible, and dozed in her rocking chair. Ruthy walked some too. She helped Mama with the dishes, sat with Molly awhile, and embroidered a bit more on her sampler.

About mid-afternoon, Papa called from the back porch. "Martha, I'd appreciate it if you'd step out here for a minute. Ruthy, you might as well come, too."

Mama jerked awake from her nap. Ruthy tossed the sampler aside and sprang up. Papa stood outside, holding a dead chicken in his hands. His jaw moved as if he were clenching his teeth.

A look of indignation spread over Mama's face. "William Donohue," Mama said. "How dare you kill that fowl! I think it's one of my best laying hens."

"I didn't kill it," Papa said. His voice shook with anger. "When I went around front just now, it was lying on the steps. Whoever's doing this must've waited until I went inside the barn and took his chance. This hen's body is still warm. Either of you hear anything?"

They hadn't.

"Where's Molly? Didn't she say anything?"

"She's been lying over there by the chimney. If she sounded, we didn't hear her," Mama said.

Papa held the chicken up by its feet and thrust it toward Mama and Ruthy. "Look at it."

The hen's head had been wrenched off. Drops of blood dripped from the raw neck.

Mama's face lost its color. She shook her head in dismay. "Wicked, wicked," she whispered. "It's a sign! I know it's a sign."

"A sign?" Papa said. "Dad-blast it, Martha! It's more than a sign. It's a straight-out threat!"

Ruthy could see her parents were angry and worried, but she didn't know what to think. Why would someone kill a chicken and leave it like that? How could killing a chicken be a threat? It didn't make sense. But since Jeremiah, nothing much in her life had made a lot of sense.

Mama looked down at Ruthy, then turned her eyes toward Papa and gave her head a small shake. "Well, there's no bringing a dead chicken back." Mama said. "Might as well dress it. I guess I can boil it and feed it to Molly. I certainly wouldn't put any part of it in my mouth. You can count on that."

After a silent supper of cornbread and milk, Papa put both hands flat on the table and cleared his throat. "I've been thinking."

"Well, I declare," Mama said with a wry smile. "Imagine that!"

Papa ignored Mama's small attempt to cheer things up. "I've been thinking it might be best for Ruthy, here, to go away somewhere for a good, long visit."

"Go away?" Ruthy said. "Why should I go away, Papa? I like it right here. With you and Mama. And Josie. Even if I haven't seen her lately."

Mama pursed her lips and shook her head. "Dear goodness," she said. "What is this world coming to? That a child can be driven from her family. I wonder who's behind this. Do you think Henry and Naomi listened to Granny after all?"

"I doubt it," Papa said. "Unless some of their kin decided to take matters into their hands. Whoever it is, I'm afraid they're not going to let up anytime soon."

He looked at Ruthy, his last child. His expression softened and his voice turned husky. "It pains me to say this, Daughter, but these goings-on make the warning pretty clear. Somebody around here believes in "an eye for an eye and a tooth for a tooth." Looks like they're bound and determined to get revenge for Jeremiah in spite of what the jury said. I'm not going to be able to protect you the way I

39

need to. Not and get my work done around the place. And if I can't do that, we'd soon starve. You can see that."

Ruthy leaned forward. "I could still stay, Papa. I could stay right near you or Mama all day. That way, you wouldn't have to worry. I'd do anything you wanted. You'd see. Please don't make me go away."

"It won't be enough," Papa said. "We'd have to be afraid all the time and I don't want you to grow up in fear. I've thought about it all day. If I had the money, I'd send you to board in an academy for young ladies. But with money as tight as it is and the crop failure last year, I just don't see my way clear to do that."

"Maybe she could go stay with Aaron and Sukey," Mama said, referring to Ruthy's older brother and his wife who lived in the next county. "With Sukey being in a family way, I'm sure she could use the help. Especially when the baby comes."

"I don't want to go stay with Aaron and Sukey," Ruthy said. "I don't know anything about taking care of babies. Besides, their house isn't even big enough for them, much less me. Remember in their last letter? Aaron said he wasn't sure where they'd even find a spot to put the baby when it came." She looked at her mother. "You remember, don't you, Mama?"

Mama nodded. "That's so."

Papa got up from the table and walked over to the fireplace. He took the poker and stirred the fire until the wood flamed up again. Turning, he said, "Aaron and Sukey were my first thought too, but they won't do. It seems to me like Ruthy ought to go somewhere where the gossip won't outrun the wagon she comes in on. No use borrowing trouble when we don't have to. And far be it from me to criticize my own daughter-in-law, but we all know that girl does like to talk."

"True," Mama said. "Sukey's ma told me, the day those children got married, that Sukey never met a secret she wasn't dying to tell."

Papa came back to the table and sat down again. "I wish Jesse didn't have such a wandering fever. If he'd stuck around instead of hooking up with those fur trappers, likely he'd be married and settled by now. Then we'd have more close family about."

"I wonder where he is, right this minute." Mama was momentarily distracted from the present situation by concern over her second son. "I guess it's mighty hard to send letters from that far away, but I sure would like to know if he's all right." She sighed and started scraping and stacking the nearest dishes, preparing them for the dishpan.

Papa nudged his bowl and cup toward Mama's busy hands. "You remember my cousin, Nathan, who married Hannah Havers, from over in Sullivan County? They moved out to Missouri several years ago. Somewhere close to a town called Springfield, I think, down towards the Arkansas line. I hear tell he's doing real fine. I've been thinking that might be a good place. New country and all." He smiled and his eyes crinkled. "I always liked old Nate. He's a real friendly feller. Did I ever tell you about the time the two of us ... ?"

"Yes, you did," Mama interrupted. "Two or three times. And I don't care if he's as friendly as two sticks in a bundle.

41

Or as rich as Midas. That's too far to send my baby." She looked at Ruthy with tears in her eyes.

"Mama, please don't call me 'baby,'" Ruthy protested. "I'm twelve years old, for heaven's sake! But you're right. That is too far to go." She sighed. "If Grandma Donohue hadn't died and gone to heaven. I could go and stay with her—if I have to go at all. I still don't see why those men, whoever they are, can't tend to their own affairs."

Papa stood. "Well, I guess they don't have enough affairs of their own to tend, so they think they have to tend ours. Chances are, they were full of meanness to begin with. All this just gave 'em an excuse for a little more. I'm not happy about sending you off, but it looks like that's the way it's going to have to be."

"Well," Mama said as she picked up a stack of dishes. "If she has to go somewhere, what about my sister, Charity? At least she lives in Tennessee. Plus, her five are all grown, so they'd have room, and she's as close-mouthed as they come. I swear, that girl never would tell me her secrets, even when we were little."

Ruthy looked hopefully at Papa. An aunt who lived in the same state would be a lot better than a cousin who lived a whole state away. Besides, she'd met Aunt Charity and liked her.

"You can write and see." Papa said. "But I have my doubts. That man of hers didn't seem any too peart the last time we got together. 'Course, that's been all of three years ago and he could have got better. But, if he's still coughing his lungs out like he was back then, it might not be a good thing."

Papa stepped closer to the door. "You get the letter ready, and I'll take it into town first thing tomorrow. I need to see Judge McIntosh, too. Let him know what's been going on.

"If Charity agrees, a visit with her would probably be best, but if she doesn't, then we'll need to think about Nathan and Hannah some more. It isn't as if Missouri is on the far side of the earth.

"Let it rest for tonight. I've got to go check the barn. Whatever happens, we're just going to have to live with it and do the best we can." He walked to the back door and stepped outside. There was nothing left to say.

RUTHY'S JOURNAL

I'm having to leave home and go far away. No Mama and Papa, no Molly, no Josie. Nobody. I'm not sure I can bear it.

Maybe Papa will change his mind. If he doesn't, I sure hope I can go to Aunt Charity's.

CHAPTER 8

Letters

Ruthy faced the following days with a heavy heart. Papa and Mama said going away was for the best and, no matter how hard she tried, Ruthy couldn't change their minds.

Papa made a special trip to town. He explained things to the judge and mailed two letters, one to Aunt Charity and one to Cousin Nathan. The second letter was "just in case," Papa said.

While they waited for answers, Mama used the time to get things ready for whatever happened. She emptied her wedding chest and began packing it. Ruthy would need some warm things for winter and extra stockings. Her shoes were worn but they'd have to do. She ought to have at least one new dress. Papa would want her to look nice when she went to church in the new place. They'd start sewing right away.

"I'll add a tuck in the hem," Mama said. "In case you get

taller. And I'll make the side seams extra wide, too. You can let them out if needs be."

"Why would I let them out?" Ruthy asked.

"In case your chest gets larger," Mama said. "It will, you know."

"Oh." She hadn't thought about that.

Ruthy collected some things, herself. The embroidered handkerchief Grandma Donohue gave her. The shiny rock from the stream near Josie's house, and her sampler, with the colored threads needed to finish it.

The chest was nearly full. She'd have to leave Mary Margaret, her old rag doll, behind. She was too big to need a doll anyway, she guessed. But she definitely had to take her journal. It would go in last, on top of everything else, so she could get to it on the trip.

Mama sewed during every spare minute. Ruthy helped by doing as many of Mama's usual chores as possible. And they talked. Seemed like Mama was bound and determined to teach Ruthy everything she would ever need to know in her whole life, before she left.

"Mama," Ruthy said. "I don't see how I'm going to remember all this. It's not like I'm leaving forever. Remember, Papa says it's only going to be a few months. And if I go to Aunt Charity's, she'll take care of me."

Mama tied a knot, bit off the thread and looked up from her work with a crooked smile. "I know. But, right now, it seems longer than that. When the boys left, I missed them, but not in the same way. I was used to them being out and about. With you, it's different."

She started another seam. "The house will be so quiet."

45

Ruthy looked at Mama as she bent over her sewing. Her mother was going to be as lonesome right here in Hawkins County as she'd be, wherever she went. Until now, Ruthy hadn't thought much about how it looked from the other side. This was hard on Mama, too.

"I'll write," she said. "You know that."

Mama looked up again. "I know," she whispered. "We'll manage." She swallowed hard and took another stitch.

They thought they might hear from Aunt Charity in three weeks or so, but six weeks went by before an answer finally came.

Dear Sister and Brother Donohue,

I hasten to say that a letter from you is always welcome. It is good to hear that everyone there is well in body. It is not so with us, at present. Husband John is doing very poorly and has done so for these past months. We find ourselves in a continual state of anxiety as to whether he will remain on this earth. I am afraid our house would not be a fit place for Ruthy under these trying circumstances. Please know that we would welcome her if things were different.

The fields hereabouts are still dry and we have little hope for rain in the near future. It seems that hard times come all too often. We will let you know how our lives work themselves out.

With trust in the goodness of Providence, I remain,

Your affectionate sister,
Charity Mullens

That was that. Aunt Charity's house was not available.

Uncle John was too sick. Maybe Cousin Nathan wouldn't be able to take her either. Maybe she'd absolutely have to stay home. Anyway, nothing bad had happened in six whole weeks. Not since they had sent the letters. Maybe it was all over. Maybe time had taken care of the whole thing just like Papa thought it might.

But it was all wishful thinking. Cousin Nathan's letter came. Papa sat is his big chair in the parlor and read the words aloud.

> We'll be glad to have Ruthy. And you might as well come along, Cousin Willie. This is a wonderful country, full of potential. If a man is willing to work, he can get along very well. The forests and waters abound in available food. I feel sure you would soon find a suitable place. As for me, I hit a spell of bad luck recently, but things are looking up and I'm confident of a strong rebound in the coming spring.
>
> We are well able to house Ruthy. Let her come when she will.
>
> Y'r cousin and friend,
>
> X
>
> Nathan Graff (his mark)

Written this 5th day of August 1837, by Jeremy Kingsolver, M.G.

Papa laid the letter on his knee. He rubbed his hand across his mouth. Mama sat very still, looking steadily at her folded hands lying idle in her lap. Ruthy moved over to stand in front of her father.

"Can I look, Papa?" she asked.

Without a word, Papa held out the single page.

Ruthy scanned the words. "It says here," Ruthy noted, "that this letter was written by Jeremy Kingsolver. Can't Cousin Nathan write?"

"No," Papa said. "He never seemed to take much to book learning and his Pa didn't insist like mine did."

Ruthy looked at the letter again. "He says we *all* might as well go over there. Why don't we, Papa? I wouldn't mind going if you and Mama came too."

"I'm afraid not, Daughter," Papa said. "New country like that is for much younger or a lot more eager men than me. I've put all the effort and money I have into this place, here, and I'm getting too far along to start over again."

"Well, I don't think anything else is going to happen," Ruthy said. "Look how long it's been. I expect things are going to be all right now."

"We'll see," Papa said. "Maybe I'll end up surprised."

RUTHY'S JOURNAL

We've had answers to both Papa's letters. Aunt Charity says I can't come there. I am so disappointed. I was counting on her. Cousin Nathan says I am welcome out where he is, but maybe I won't have to go. Maybe the meanness is over. I wonder what kind of bad luck Cousin N. meant in his letter.

CHAPTER 9

Last Straw

For more than two weeks, Cousin Nathan's letter sat on the mantel, silently demanding an answer. Every single day, Ruthy looked up at it and crossed her fingers, making a wish that Papa's answer would finally turn out to be "thank you, but she isn't coming after all." Every single day, life in the Donohue house went on as normally as possible. All three of them tried hard to talk about ordinary things. But the possibility of something bad happening again lurked in every dark corner of the house and hid behind every tree. It was always there.

"Papa," Ruthy finally said one night at supper, "Don't you think it's time to write Cousin Nathan and tell him I needn't come, after all?"

Papa glanced toward the mantel where the letter still stood, a spot of white against the smoke-stained chimney stones. "I'm still of two minds about that," he said. "I admit

49

to being surprised that nothing else has happened. But whoever is responsible may be saving up to do something worse."

Mama picked up a bowl of hominy she'd cooked, along with a slab of ham, for their meal, and silently offered a second serving to Papa, raising her eyebrows as a question. He shook his head.

"Well," Mama said, setting the bowl back down, "one way or the other, I hope you see your way clear before much longer. Living on pins and needles is wearing me down."

That night, Molly woke the whole family up with loud, frantic barking. Ruthy heard her father get out of bed and pull on his pants. "What is it, Papa?" she called.

"Probably a fox after the hens," Papa answered. "I'll check." His footsteps sounded all the way down the stairs and across to the back door. The latch clicked as he lifted it and looked out.

"Dear Lord in Heaven," he shouted. "It's a fire." Ruthy heard the door hit the wall as her father flung it back. "Martha, Ruthy! Fire at the barn. Get up. Fill the buckets. Hurry!"

Ruthy and Mama ran outside in their nightgowns to see a large fire blazing at the barn. Smoke hung heavy in the air. Mama grabbed one bucket and thrust another into Ruthy's hand. "Run, child. Don't wait for me."

Ruthy hitched up her nightgown and tore to the spring as fast as her legs would move. She filled the bucket and ran toward the barn, coughing as she went through the smoke.

What would they do if they lost the barn? All Papa's tools. The wagon. And Buck and Betsy! What about them?

And the cows, the pigs. Had they got out? What if they hadn't? What if they burned up?

Heart pounding, she raced through the haze, looking for Papa.

There he was. At the haystack. The barn wasn't on fire. It was the hay. Not the barn. It was the hay. Her shoulders sagged briefly in relief as she hurried on.

Papa stabbed the pitchfork over and over into the blazing stack, flinging bits of hay right and left, away from the barn's wooden logs. He was coughing, too.

"Here's some water, Papa," Ruthy shouted. The smoke bit the back of her throat worse with every breath.

"Wet down the wall of the barn," Papa gasped between coughs. "Hurry." He pointed to the section nearest the haystack. "There."

Ruthy splashed the water where Papa pointed. She could hear the frightened animals calling. Turning back, she yelled, "What about Buck and Betsy? And the others?"

"No time," Papa panted. "Got to move this hay." He tossed another smoking forkful away and looked up. "Don't stand there!" he shouted. "Move!"

Still worried about the animals, Ruthy turned back to the spring. She met Mama on the way. "Papa said to wet down the barn wall."

Mama nodded. She removed a wet rag she'd picked up somewhere to hold over her nose and mouth and handed it to Ruthy. "Take this and use it. Try not to breathe in any more smoke than you can help," she gasped.

It seemed like they fought the fire for an awfully long time. When it was over, Papa looked near to collapse.

51

Holding on to the pitchfork, he bent over and coughed in great tearing gasps. Bits of blackened hay, some still smoking, were scattered far and wide. A smoky haze hung over the valley. All their winter feed was gone.

But they still had the barn. It was only slightly charred on one side. Somehow, they could make do, so long as they still had the barn and the animals.

Mama leaned on the handle of the hoe she'd used to separate the last smoldering bundles. Her hair hung down in sweaty strings.

Ruthy sprawled on the ground, her nightgown so black with falling ash and spattered mud that she thought it might not ever be white again. Her whole body ached. She looked at the scorched barn and the nervous animals they had finally managed to move outside. Everything stank of smoke and water and burnt hay. It was enough to make a person gag.

A faint light showed in the east by the time the small family staggered back to the house and collapsed on the benches around the table.

Ruthy looked at her father. His face was drawn with worry and exhaustion. For the first time in her life, Ruthy thought Papa looked old. "How come the hay caught fire?" she asked.

"Let's hope it was lightning," Mama said. She pushed her hair back and began to work it into a thick plait to keep it out of her face.

Ruthy knew better. It couldn't have been lightning. There hadn't been a cloud in the sky. She turned toward Papa.

He shook his head and rubbed one smoke-stained hand across his mouth, leaving a gray smear behind. "It must have been set. I can't think of any other cause."

Ruthy's heart sank. She'd known it, somehow, even before she asked. The meanness had begun again. And, this time, it was even worse than before. This time, the whole family was suffering because of her. And Papa looked old.

When she thought about it later, it seemed her next action was the best and most grown-up thing she had ever done. She rose from the table, walked to the washbasin, scrubbed her grimy hands and retrieved the writing paper, pen and ink from its place on a shelf. Laying them in front of her father, she said, "Papa, it's time to answer Cousin Nathan's letter. Tell him I'll be coming to stay as soon as we find someone to take me."

Papa never said a word. He just sat there and stared.

"Are you sure?" Mama asked. "Are you absolutely sure? You won't feel we've turned you out?"

"Yes, Mama," Ruthy answered. "I'm more sure than I've ever been about anything. If I don't go, what will happen next? Will they burn the barn? Our house? Kill Buck or Betsy? I have to go. You can see that. I have to."

Still silent, Papa rose slowly and moved stiffly to wash his hands too. Then he sat down, opened the inkbottle, dipped the pen into the ink, tapped it slightly to shake off the extra liquid, and began to write.

So much has happened, it's almost more than I can write about. We had a fire and it was awful. Everything still smells of smoke and there's a big black spot on the ground where the haystack was.

But I can't think about that anymore. I have to think about going away. Only a few more days until I leave for a faraway land, to live with people I don't know at all. Papa says I'll remember Cousin Nathan when I see him, but what if I don't?

Leaving home is the hardest thing I've ever had to do, in my whole life.

CHAPTER 10

Hard Money

After Papa mailed the second letter to Cousin Nathan, he went to town three more times. Each time, he checked to see if anyone knew of a wagon going to Missouri. No one did. Each time, Papa brought home something for Ruthy's trip. The first time, it was a bottle of ink and some writing paper. The second time, he took a year-old calf with him and brought home a handful of silver coins.

"I told the stock man I had to have hard money, so I didn't get as much as I wanted for the calf," he told Mama. "But I've never trusted all those paper bills people have been throwing around. And it looks like I was right. I heard rumors in town about banks failing all over the country."

"Failing?" Mama asked. "I don't understand."

"Well, I'm not sure I do either. But, from what I pieced together out of all I heard today, this is what I think happens.

"People like us hear rumors of hard times coming. They

55

read about banks closing in other parts of the country and about people losing all the money they had saved. Pretty soon, everybody else starts to worry about their money. What if their bank closes, too? So they go down to the bank and ask for what they have in there—for safety's sake.

"And they want real money. Silver and gold; not those worthless paper notes. Of course, the banks don't have enough hard money on hand to satisfy everyone. They never do. So the banks have to close. And all the people who had money on deposit and weren't first in line are out of luck. No money."

"None?" Mama asked. Her face looked fearful.

"Not one red cent. Right now, I'm sorta glad I've never had enough to need a bank."

Mama heaved a big sigh. "So we're all right?"

Papa's laugh sounded harsh. "As right as we ever are. Be glad we have some hams in the smoke house and corn in the barn."

"Think what would have happened if the barn had burned down," Mama said. She wrapped her arms in her apron.

Papa turned to Ruthy. "These are for you, Daughter," he said, holding four coins out on the palm of his hand. "In case there's an emergency while you're far away. You can tell from what I just said that money isn't easy to come by right now. Times are hard and I expect they'll get harder. Don't use any of this unless you absolutely have to."

Ruthy took the coins. They all looked about the same except two were bigger. All four were silver with a lady's head on the front. She wore a funny-looking cap. Thirteen stars circled around the edge. She turned one over. The back had an eagle with a long neck.

"The big ones are worth fifty cents apiece," Papa said. "That's a lot of money these days. Some men have to work hard for more than half a day to make that much. The smaller ones are quarters—twenty-five cents."

Ruthy had never held so much money at one time in her whole life. It seemed like a fortune. She couldn't imagine how she could spend all that. Sometimes she got a penny for Christmas or her birthday and she bought candy, but this was sure a lot more than a penny.

"Give them here, Ruthy," Mama said. "We'll sew them inside the band of your best petticoat. The one with the embroidery at the bottom. You won't have to wash it as often, so nobody is likely to know they're there. Come watch, so you'll know exactly where they are."

Ruthy looked on as Mama made a separate pocket for each coin on the inside band of her Sunday petticoat. "See? This way, if you need one, you can get it without disturbing the others. Just snip this double thread, here, on the back-side of the band, and pull."

When Papa came home the third time, he announced, "We're in luck. I found a family heading to Missouri. And, would you believe it? They're actually going to Greene County. Maybe things are starting to go our way for a change."

Mama's hand flew to her chest. Her fingers were crossed. "I certainly hope so. Who are they? Anybody we know?"

"No, but we know somebody who does. James and

Kizzie Perkins, from over in Sullivan County. Not far from where Aaron's Sukey grew up. They seem real nice. She's kin somehow to Purdy McFee's wife's sister," he went on. "A jolly sort of woman. Young."

He looked at Ruthy. "They have room for you and they promised me they'd see you got to Nate and Hannah's all safe and sound. You'll be expected to help out for your keep but I'd want you to do that anyway. Only problem is, they want to leave by the end of the week. That doesn't give us much time, but I told them you'd be ready."

CHAPTER 11

Hard Lesson

Papa's announcement hung heavy in the air like a low thundercloud before a storm. Mama grabbed the back of a nearby chair so hard her knuckles turned white. Ruthy just stood there and swiveled her head, looking from one parent to the other.

"I was right, wasn't I, Martha? She *is* ready, isn't she?" Papa asked. "If she isn't, what's lacking? Let's get to it. This is probably her best—maybe her only—chance this season."

"Nothing's lacking." Mama looked around. "At least, nothing that can't be finished up right away." Her hands strayed to her apron, smoothing it mindlessly. "I know it sounds foolish, William, but I kept hoping you wouldn't find anyone."

"Well, I did," Papa said. "But speaking of what's lacking—there is one thing." He turned to Ruthy. "It came to me on the way back from town. I should have done it sooner. I don't know why I didn't."

"What, Papa?"

"You'll see." He picked up his long rifle, powder horn, and bullet pouch. "We'll be out behind the barn, Martha."

Puzzled, Ruthy followed her father as he strode from the house. "Why are you taking the gun, Papa? Has a varmint been poking around?"

"Not that I know of," Papa said. He kept walking.

"Then why are you taking the gun?" Ruthy asked again. "Do you think the bad men might be hiding out there?"

No answer. Papa stepped up his pace. Ruthy hurried to keep up.

They walked past the smokehouse, rounded the corner of the cow pen and stopped just beyond the back of the barn. The smell of burnt hay still lingered.

Papa rested his rifle butt on the ground and looked about as if expecting to find something new. Finally, he said, "You see those trees over yonder, Ruthy? I left them standing so the stock would always have a shade. I've been glad about that ever since."

"I know that, Papa. You told me before. Is that what you brought me out here for? To tell me that again? I don't understand."

Papa drew a long breath. "Naw, I'm just talking."

He lifted his rifle and sighted along the barrel, then lowered it slightly. "I intend to show you how to load and shoot this gun the right way. I taught the boys when they were younger than you are but somehow I never got around to it with you. Seems like the boys were always mine to teach.

60

under her breath. She wondered what he'd do if she just kept on walking. Not quite daring to find out, she trudged back.

"Here. It's your turn. Let's see how much you learned." Papa thrust the rifle into Ruthy's hands. She held the weapon carefully and looked at it, mistrust in every line of her body.

"Check to make sure it isn't cocked," Papa said.

It wasn't.

"Put it up to your shoulder and try to aim it."

The rifle was as heavy as she remembered from before. The long barrel wavered when she tried to point it.

"It looks like you'll need to rest it on something," Papa said. "Come over here to the cowpen and rest the barrel on the top rail. See if that helps."

Ruthy did as he suggested. It was better. She wished it hadn't been. She wished the rifle would be too much for her to handle safely. That way, she still might not have to shoot this gun.

But she was out of luck. Papa kept after her and kept after her. He made her practice everything several times. Loading wasn't so hard. She spilled some gunpowder once but not very much. The hard part was pulling the trigger. The first time, she shook so bad and aimed so poorly that Papa said the bullet might have gone into the next county for all he knew. It was hard to hold still, what with that scary flash right in front of her eyes, the loud noise and the awful jolt as the rifle butt kicked back into her shoulder.

Her arm would probably never work right again and Papa didn't even seem to care. All he said was to snug the gun in tighter against her shoulder. Then it wouldn't kick so much.

By the time he was satisfied, Ruthy's arms trembled from exhaustion. Powder flashes blackened her face and her ears rang. Still, she could do it. She could load, aim, look to be sure, cock, and fire.

Toward the end, Mama came out to watch. She seemed to stand there for an age before finally announcing, "I believe it's time to wash up for supper. From the looks of things, both of you have wasted enough lead."

Thankful to stop, Ruthy checked to see that the gun was uncocked and gave it back to her father.

He patted her shoulder. "Good work, Ruthy," he said. "Now I can send you off with a restful conscience."

Ruthy nodded, glad he was satisfied. After today, even the trip to Missouri didn't sound so bad. If she could face this, she could probably face anything.

RUTHY'S JOURNAL

I found out today that I leave at week's end. This afternoon Papa made me learn to shoot his gun. I didn't think it necessary, but he insisted, and Mama never said a word. My ears still ring from all the noise. My shoulder's sore, too. I expect to be black and blue by morning. It puzzles me why men and boys think shooting is such a great thing.

CHAPTER 12

Leaving

On Leaving Day, the Donohue family started for Rogersville long before the sun rose over the hills. They had to travel nearly five miles, around the end of Stone Mountain, over a rise, down a long slope and through a gap between two small hills before they could see the court-house belfry rising above the trees. Geese flew overhead and the air held a hint of chill.

Ruthy, wearing a cape and bonnet, huddled between Mama and Papa for the last time. Her chest ached, likely caused by the heavy weight that used to be her heart. A big, stubborn lump clogged her throat. It wouldn't go away, no matter how hard she swallowed. Seemed like every time she thought she'd lived through the worst day of her life, something else even worse came along. At least the prodigal son they talked about in the Bible went to a faraway land because he wanted to. It wasn't because mean people made him go away.

"Wouldn't it be nice if you saw Jesse, out in Missouri?" Mama's hearty tone sounded forced.

"Yes, it would," Ruthy said. If her younger brother, the one with the wandering foot, turned up nearby, going away would be a lot better.

"Don't pin your hopes on that," Papa said. "Because you'd likely be out of luck. 'Fore he left, he told me he'd try to hook up with some mountain men and go as far west as he could. I doubt he stopped in Missouri."

Mama shook her head in disbelief. "I never thought, in my wildest mind, that I'd lose two of my young'uns to way out yonder and beyond."

"Remember, it won't be forever, Mama," Ruthy said. "As soon as possible, I'll come back and everything will be the same as before. You'll see."

Mama just shook her head.

After what seemed like a much shorter trip than usual, the wagon pulled over the last rise. They were nearly there. The rock in Ruthy's chest turned into a heart again and began thudding against her ribs.

Papa drove west all the way down Main Street, past the big courthouse with the tall white columns, by the Hale Springs Inn, and on beyond the cemetery.

Mama sighed. She reached for Ruthy's hand. "I keep trying to think if there's anything else I need to tell you, but I guess not. You're a good girl and you've been brought up right. Remember to say your prayers and practice your reading. And don't forget to be as helpful as you can, no matter where you are." Her chuckle sounded awkward. "And, for dear goodness' sake, finish that sampler! I can't think how it's taken you so long."

There were only four wagons in the camp outside of town.

"I thought there'd be more," Mama said. "I wonder who the others belong to."

Papa pulled up near the campsite. Several people worked around the wagons. Men were feeding horses and mules. An older boy carried a bucket toward the creek. Ruthy noticed a plump, pleasant-looking, young woman squatting by the fire. The woman saw the new arrivals and turned her head to call, "Jimmy, they're here."

When James Perkins walked out from behind the nearest wagon, Ruthy couldn't help but stare. He was the tallest, thinnest man she'd ever seen and he wore a ragged gray hat that sagged down on one side. He towered over Papa when they shook hands.

"Howdy, folks. You're here in good time," Mr. Perkins said. "This our young lady passenger?" he asked, looking at Ruthy.

"Yes, this is Ruthy, and this is my wife, Martha."

Mr. Perkins tipped his hat to Mama. "Ma'am, it's good to meet you. Get down and come over to the fire. I think Kizzie still has some coffee in the pot." He smiled and Ruthy saw a gap where a front tooth had been. "She can't hardly wait to say hello to Miss Ruthy, here."

They walked toward the friendly-faced woman, who, by this time, had stood and straightened her skirt. "It's good to see you folks," she said, nodding and smiling her welcome.

69

Mama nodded back and turned to Ruthy. "This is our daughter, Ruthy. I hope she won't be any trouble."

"Ain't you a pretty thing!" Kizzie said. "I love your hair. I've always wished mine would be something besides plain brown." She pushed her hair away from her face. "But we don't always get what we want, do we?"

She turned to Mama. "Don't you worry about a thing. We'll get along just fine. I'll be glad to have another woman on the trip. She can help me keep these men and boys in line." She waved her hand at the workers around the wagons. Ruthy hadn't noticed until then, but there wasn't another woman or girl in sight.

"Are we the only ones?" she asked.

"Well, yes, if you don't count Ophelia. She's my little'un, over there in the basket under the wagon. Actually, she's the real reason I was so glad to have you come along. She's a colicky baby and can really be fretful when she sets her mind to it. You'll be a big help with her."

Ruthy's heart sank a bit at that. She'd never taken care of a baby. And she especially didn't know anything about colicky, fretful babies. She'd better say something right now. Then, if Mrs. Perkins didn't want her, they could wait and find another wagon.

"Mrs. Perkins," she began, only to be interrupted.

"Honey, I ain't been 'Miz Perkins' for hardly a year yet. And I still ain't used to it. Why don't you just call me 'Kizzie.' That way, it'll be almost like you was my little sister or something. It'll be a lot easier. And you can call him 'Perk.'" She nodded her head toward her tall, thin husband. "Everybody else does." She put an arm around Ruthy's shoulders and walked her toward the nearest wagon. "Come meet Ophelia."

Ruthy couldn't see she had much choice but to go where the welcoming arm steered her. And by the time she had smiled at the baby and said a few nice things—most of which weren't even true—the moment had passed.

Back at the fire, Mama patted her daughter's back and whispered, "She seems kind. You'll learn."

Papa and Mr. Perkins—she couldn't bring herself to think of him as 'Perk' yet—loaded her chest in the biggest wagon and came back to the fire.

"You'll head towards Nashville?" Papa asked.

"Yes," Mr. Perkins said. "Then angle up through Kentucky, towards the northwest. Probably turn west when we hit Hopkinsville. I hear tell that's about the best way to go."

"I've heard that too," Papa said. He spat and shifted his feet, staring at the fire. Finally, he straightened his shoulders and looked toward Mama. She nodded.

He turned to the young couple. "We'd best get on home and let you get moving." He laid a hand on Ruthy's shoulder and squeezed gently. "If this young'un gives you any trouble, don't think twice about settin' her straight. We expect her to behave."

Ruthy ducked her head and scuffed her shoe in the dirt. Papa made it sound like she was a child, needing to be minded.

"I'm not a bit worried, Mr. Donohue," Kizzie said. "We'll do fine." She looked at the baby in her arms and jiggled her a bit. "Won't we, Feelie? We'll do just fine." She laid the little one on her shoulder and nodded to Mama again. "Don't you worry neither, Miz Donohue. We'll watch over her and see her safe."

Mama pursed her quivering lips tightly. She reached out to give Ruthy a last hug and stumbled back to the Donohue wagon.

Papa cupped Ruthy's cheek gently in his hand. "Don't forget to write. Your mother will want to hear." He cleared his throat. "And I will too."

Tears welled in Ruthy's eyes. "I won't, Papa," she whispered, blinking rapidly. "But I'll be back before you know it and it will all be like I never left."

And that was it. Papa walked to the wagon and climbed up beside Mama. Clicking to Buck and Betsy, he drove away, raising one hand in farewell. Mama kept turning around, waving, until they drove out of sight.

RUTHY'S JOURNAL

Sept. 23, 1837
Near Knoxville

Going To Missouri

It's been three whole days since I've written a word. There never seems to be any time. Traveling is harder than I thought. Especially with only two of us to do the cooking. The men made a deal with Perk for Kizzie to cook for everyone. No wonder she was glad to have me here to help. We try to fix enough food at night to have some for the next day's nooning. Especially beans. We're always soaking beans. In the mornings, we fry salt pork and make coffee and lots of corncakes. That, plus molasses, keeps us going. It is a treat when we have biscuits on the Sabbath. Or when one of the men has a successful hunt. Perk is saving money for land and doesn't want to buy extras in the towns we pass.

Here are the people in our train besides me:
James Perkins, Kizzie, & Ophelia
Mr. Alexander Grogan & his son, Will
Mr. John Keeter
Mr. Hannibal Lewis and his brother, Daniel

Mr. Grogan and Will have two wagons—one for them and one for things to sell. They hope to open a store somewhere in Missouri.

Mr. Keeter is by himself. If he finds the right spot to settle, he'll come back for his family.

The Lewis brothers ride together. They're only going with us as far as Kentucky. They have kin there. I'm not sure just where.

Too dark to keep writing.

73

CHAPTER 13

Letter Home

Sept. 27, 1837

Dear Mama and Papa,

We have been on the road for eight whole days and are stopped at a place called Crab Orchard for repairs. Two of the spokes on Mr. Lewis' wagon broke. Today turned off windy but dry, so we took the opportunity to wash, not knowing when we'd be able to again. And it was a good thing we did. The wet diaper cloths have been dried so many times, they were nearly stiff. They really needed washing.

Kizzie and I get along very well, which is more than I can say for my acquaintance with Will Grogan. He is a braggart and showoff, but mindful of this past year, I am trying to bear it in silence. Kizzie says I should learn to laugh and tease him back. I try to follow her advice.

Baby Feelie is not yet easy with me. Nor I with her, if truth be told. She cries when I hold her and wants her mama. I'm making her a rattle from a gourd I found. Maybe she will like me better then. You would be proud of my cooking. I can make biscuits now. And haven't let the beans burn a single time.

How is everything there? Any more trouble? How is Molly? Is she walking better? Please give her a pat from me. Also, Buck and Betsy. And if you see Josie, tell her I send greetings.

Kizzie says you can direct a letter in care of Ste. Genevieve, Missouri, post office, as Perk plans to stop there. I am well, but long to hear from you.

Your loving daughter,
Ruth Ann Donohue

P.S. I seem to be something of a spectacle when I sit to use pen and ink. Perk can sign his name. I'm not sure about the Lewis brothers but I think the Grogans are the only others in this train who truly read and write. Will says I know more than any woman needs to. I told him our family always set great store by learning.

Papa, the little writing board you made is quite nice and was a real surprise. I found it the first time I got paper from the chest. Thank you.

R.

CHAPTER 14

Challenged

"Wake up, Ruthy. I need your help. Right now." Perk's voice startled Ruthy out of a sound sleep. She peered from her warm cocoon of quilts inside the wagon. It was quite dark and felt like the middle of the night. The shape of Perk's head and shoulders showed black against the dim light of a new moon. "What's wrong?" she asked.

"Kizzie's sick. She puked awhile ago and is burning up with fever. Now Feelie's commenced to yell. I can't take care of both of them. I'd appreciate it mightily if you'd get up." He disappeared.

Ruthy rubbed her eyes and struggled from the tangle of quilts where she slept on top of the chests, between the trunks. Shivering, she grabbed the first piece of cover that came to hand, wrapped it around her shoulders and climbed to the ground.

"Girl, come on over here and get Feelie!" Perk's low voice sounded like he really wanted to yell.

Ruthy hurried to drag the small traveling cradle out from under the wagon, where it lay next to Kizzie. How could that much noise come from such a small body? She picked up the protesting infant. Pee-you! She was wet! Really wet.

The diapering cloths. Where were they? Oh, yes, in a basket right behind the wagon seat where Kizzie could reach them during the day. Jiggling the squawling Ophelia, and trying to shush her, Ruthy walked to the front of the wagon to get a dry clout. She stood on tiptoe and stretched, but she couldn't reach them. And she certainly couldn't climb up with the baby in her arms.

Sighing in frustration, she laid the baby on the ground atop the quilt she'd been using for a wrap and stepped up on one of the wagon spokes. The basket of folded cloths was right where she remembered. She grabbed the top one, hopped down, and turned to where Ophelia lay, kicking and screaming.

Now what? Ruthy wished she'd paid more attention to mothers and babies back home. She lifted the skirt of the baby's dress. It couldn't be all that hard. She could do this. Anything to stop Feelie from crying. A single button in the middle held the wet triangular clout together. Very carefully, trying to use only the tips of her fingers, Ruthy unbuttoned the two corners. She held her breath and pulled the wet cloth away. Did she imagine it or were the cries a bit softer?

She unfolded the dry cloth and spread it out. The soft

triangle had two buttonholes in the far corners and a single button on the middle point. Someone had taken a lot of pains to make such nice clouts. Ruthy had a vague memory of some woman she'd seen using straight pins at the corners.

Awkwardly, Ruthy worked the cloth under the baby's bottom. She pulled the short corner up between the legs, then fastened each of the other two corners to the button in the middle.

There! Now, maybe Feelie would stop crying.

But she didn't. If anything, she got louder again.

Walking while carrying her didn't work. Humming a song didn't work. Patting her back didn't help either.

Perk looked up from his crouching position by Kizzie. "That young'un's going to wake the whole train. Probably already has. Can't you do any better than that?"

Ruthy kept trying, jiggling and humming and patting all at once.

"Sounds like you could use some help." A man's voice came from behind the next wagon. It was Mr. Keeter. He walked out of the shadows, pulling his suspenders over his shoulders as he came. He looked first toward Perk. "Perkins, what's wrong? Is your woman bad sick? Do I need to ride for help?"

"Kizzie says not," Perk said. "She's pretty sure it's just something she ate. She says wait till morning before getting things all stirred up."

"Well, I'm here if you need me," Mr. Keeter answered.

He turned to Ruthy. "Purty fussy, ain't she? Hand her here a minute."

Ruthy hesitated.

"I've had seven of my own, four living. I've dandled quite a few."

Reassured, Ruthy gave up the baby and, at that moment, realized she was wearing only her shift. Face hot with embarrassment, she took two quick steps, snatched up the quilt and wrapped it around her again, clutching it close.

"Got a clean cloth handy?" Mr. Keeter patted the baby's back with his big, work-worn hand and murmured something. Ophelia's yells subsided to an occasional hiccup. Ruthy wondered what he'd done that she hadn't.

"I guess so," Ruthy said. "What for? I already gave her dry linen."

"For a sop," Mr. Keeter said. "She needs something to suck on. Why don't you mix a bit of them molasses in a cup with some water and dip the cloth in it. She'll like it. You'll see."

Ruthy hurried to follow Mr. Keeter's suggestion.

"Sit down there." He pointed to a grassy spot near the fire. "Here." He handed Ophelia back to Ruthy and dipped a corner of the cloth in the sweet water.

When the sop brushed her lips, the baby opened her mouth and began to suck. Ruthy felt the baby's whole body relax.

"She'll go to sleep soon, I reckon," Keeter said.

Ruthy looked at the calm, quiet infant. "How did you know to do that?"

"By watching my wife. She's a knowing sort of woman. Especially with little ones," Mr. Keeter answered over his shoulder as he walked back to his own wagon. "Now you know a little bit too."

"Not enough," Ruthy thought. She yawned and settled in to wait for morning. "Not near enough."

CHAPTER 15

Journal Entry 11

Near Sparta, Tenn.

We're down the far side of the Cumberland Mountains at last! My heart was in my throat as we came down those steep slopes. I thought they'd never end. Tying a log to the back of the wagon for an extra brake helped a lot. But it was still chancy enough that Kizzie and I had to get out sometimes, along with the baby, while the men held onto ropes tied to the back axle.

Kizzie has recovered. Perk mashed up some bits of charcoal into a powder and mixed it with some milk. Kizzie drank it and said it made her stomach feel better. I must remember that.

I think Feelie likes me a bit more since I had to take care of her. She laughs when I shake her rattle and doesn't fuss as much when I hold her.

81

CHAPTER 16

Longing

"She's asleep at last. Let's hope she stays that way for awhile," Kizzie said, returning from the wagon where she'd been nursing Ophelia. She sat down on the ground opposite the cook fire's smoke and looked at Ruthy. "Here you are, putting words down in that little book again. I thought you was watching supper."

The wagons were stopped for the night. The sun hung low in the west and a bright ray seemed to set Ruthy's hair afire. She had been alternating between stirring the stew, made from squirrels Mr. Keeter shot, and catching up in her journal.

"I can do both. It's hard to find time to write. I have to wait until we stop moving and then there's chores. This seemed like a good time."

"What in the world do you find to write about?"

"I'm trying to keep a record of our trip," Ruthy explained. She closed the book, laid it on a nearby log and capped her ink bottle. It was time to give the stew another stir.

A stray breeze blew smoke from the cook fire in her face. She squinted her nose and stepped sideways to avoid the biting smell. "This way, when I see Mama and Papa again, I'll remember all the things I want to tell them."

"Do you write about me?" Kizzie asked. "And the rest of us?"

"Sometimes," Ruthy said. "But never anything bad. Would you like to hear what I just wrote?"

Kizzie nodded. "I'll tend the fire."

Ruthy opened her journal, marked the place with her finger, and looked up. "You won't tell the others, will you? I wouldn't want them all to know what I put down."

"I won't tell." Kizzie said. She paused. "Well, I might say something to Perk, but no one else."

Reassured, Ruthy began to read:

"We passed through Nashville today. Seems like we've been on the road forever and we still aren't out of our own state! I never realized it would take so long to get to Missouri. I am tired of riding in the wagon, tired of walking, and heartily tired of Will Grogan and his bothersome ways. Always making jokes and asking questions. Kizzie says he only wants to be friends but I just wish he'd leave me alone.

I cooked one of Papa's favorite dishes for supper last night, mixing salt pork and molasses with the beans and baking them in Mr. Keeter's Dutch oven. He kindly lent it to us for use during the journey. I think everyone liked what I made.

The land around here is so different from home. The hills aren't so steep, for one thing and the roads don't wind around nearly as much.

Ruthy closed the journal and looked anxiously at her friend. "You said you wouldn't tell. You won't, will you?"

Kizzie laughed. "You mean you don't want Will to know you wrote about him? He might like knowing that."

"You promised, Kizzie. You promised."

"Naw, I won't say anything. But I still think you ought to smile a bit when he's around. You'll never catch a man, the way you're going.

"Don't rush me," Ruthy said. "I'm not quite thirteen. I have time. Mama didn't marry till she was eighteen."

"That doesn't mean she didn't take an interest before." Kizzie poked Ruthy in the ribs with the stirring spoon. "By the time I was your age, I'd had three boyfriends. And I married old Perk, there, at sixteen." She stooped to shift a log in the fire and check the cookpot again.

"'Course," she continued. "Look where that got me. I ain't sorry I'm with Perk. He's a good man. But when I watch you, I do wish I could have learned to read a bit and maybe write my name. We never had no school, out where I grew up." Her voice filled with longing. "You're lucky."

Ruthy looked at Kizzie with renewed interest. Reading and writing weren't lucky things. All her family could do that. She hadn't even realized her friend didn't know how.

"I could teach you," she offered. "It isn't hard."

"For you, maybe. I'm not so sure about me. Still, I may take you up on your offer, if we can ever find time." Kizzie took a last look at the stew. "Our victuals are ready. Call the men, will you? But not too loud. I don't want Feelie to wake."

RUTHY'S JOURNAL

I must remember to be grateful for knowing how to read and write. Until today, I didn't know it mattered that much. I certainly hope Will Grogan will stay away from me. It would make life so much easier. I never know what to say to him.

CHAPTER 17

Second Letter Home

Oct. 9, 1837
Near Hopkinsville, Kentucky

Dear Mama and Papa,

This is my second letter. I hope you got the first. We are out of Tennessee at last, are camped at the Patterson place on Little River, and seem set to stay for two or three days. We need to rest the stock and make some repairs. The Lewis brothers stop here as planned. Mrs. Patterson is their sister.

Some days ago, we had quite a scare. Kizzie was sick all night. We were all worried but she took some charcoal powder and recovered enough by morning for us to travel. Baby Feelie wakened the whole camp with her pitiful cries. It was a long night.

We had a soaking rain soon after we left Nashville,

86

which, as you can imagine, added much misery to our journey. It was hard to keep the cooking fire burning. Plus, one of the Grogan wagons got stuck and we had a time getting it moving again. Kizzie and I wanted to take shelter somewhere and wait until the heavens closed and the roads dried out a bit, but Perk would not. He is determined to push on and the other men agree.

I much doubt he would have stopped now, except Mr. Patterson has some smithing tools and the Grogans need to re-shoe their mules.

The Pattersons have a nice place. The house and barn are large and Mrs. Patterson has invited us to take our noon meals with them. She is a very good cook. Nearly as good as you are, Mama. Today we had turnip soup, with carrots and lots of spices in it, and chess pie for dessert. She said she always makes that pie when company comes. I asked her for the receipt and wrote it down so I can show you when we are back together.

Kizzie, Feelie, and I spent yesterday afternoon indoors with Mrs. P. and will do so again today. She seems to enjoy having us. You'll be happy to know I stitch on my sampler while we visit. I have finished the entire second and third lines: "In learning I take great delight; Beauty soon will fade away, . . ."

I continue in good health and hope both of you do the same. And that reminds me to ask you, Mama, if you would send me receipts for some of your best medicines. Since Kizzie fell ill back there, I've been worried. I shudder to think what little help I could give a sick person, by myself. Also, if there is room on the page, please send the receipt for cider cake. I tried to tell it to Kizzie and Mrs. P. but couldn't remember it all. Papa, I hope this letter doesn't cost you too much.

Your loving daughter,
Ruth Ann Donohue

P.S. Perk just came back to the wagon. He still plans to cross the Mississippi at St. Genevieve. I will look for your letter there.

CHAPTER 18

Hard Encounter

After the wagons left the comfort of the Patterson place, travel seemed extra hard to Ruthy. She missed sitting at a table to eat and spending afternoons doing handwork and visiting.

Each day, she asked Perk how far they still had to go. Finally, he said, "I don't know. It depends. We'll get there when we get there. If you're so all-fired interested, go ask Grogan. He has a whole book of maps he keeps poking in my face. All I know right now is, our next town is Salem and pretty soon after that, we cross the Ohio."

"I'm sorry for pestering you," Ruthy said. She hadn't known Mr. Grogan had maps. "I'll ask him." She climbed out the back of the Perkins wagon and hopped to the ground. She'd learned early in the trip how to do that. If you timed it just right, held on to the back end and trotted a few steps before turning loose, you could get down easy, without the wagon having to stop.

Mr. Keeter's wagon came next in line behind the Perkins, then Mr. Grogan's. Will's wagon came last. He didn't like eating dust every day, but he was the youngest and that's where he stayed.

"Tired of riding, Miss Ruthy?" Mr. Keeter asked from his perch.

"Yes, I am," Ruthy said. She fell in step with the Keeter wagon. "Don't you ever get tired of just sitting there and driving all day? I would."

"Well, I do and I don't," Mr. Keeter said. "I get a little saddle-sore, so to speak, but this bench cushion the wife made helps that. By now, my horses are pretty well used to following Perkins, so I don't have to work much on the reins. That gives me time to look around."

Ruthy walked a bit faster as the horses moved down a slope. "What do you look for? Anything special?" she asked.

"Oh, I look at the land and think about how it's like and different from what I've knowed before. I watch the growing things and see how they're doing. I think what I'd do if I lived around here." Mr. Keeter chuckled. "And I talk to the missus in my head. I tell her all the things I'd say if she was sitting here. Don't sound like much, maybe, but it passes the time."

Ruthy raised her hand in a temporary leave-taking. "At least it does that. See you later," she said, and waited for the first Grogan wagon to move even with where she stood.

"Hi, Mr. Grogan. You feel like talking a bit?"

"Sure, child. I'll be glad of a visit. My own company certainly isn't all that interesting right now."

Ruthy turned to keep pace with the Grogan mules. They were big critters, both of them. Much taller than Mr. Keeter's sturdy horses. And those long ears looked so comical.

"Perk says you have some maps and I should look at them instead of asking him about everything."

"You must be talking about my atlas. It's a whole book of maps. I probably have the only copy in these parts. Comes out of Philadelphia. It shows all the roads and distances for the whole United States. Steamboat and canal routes too. It's really something. I figure I can sell it for a tidy sum when I get my store up and running."

Ruthy's shoulders sagged. "Oh, I didn't know it was something to sell. I thought maybe it was yours and I could look at it."

Mr. Grogan twitched his reins to remove a pesky fly biting one of the mules' sides. "There, Jubal" he called. "That better?" The mule snorted and the storekeeper turned back to Ruthy. "It is for sale, but that won't keep us from looking at it, if we're careful. Thing is, it's in the other wagon. I'll tell you what. Go back there —," he tilted his head to the back, "and tell Will I said to get it out for you next time we stop."

Ruthy hadn't counted on having to talk to Will. "Couldn't you tell him?"

"Go on, child," Mr. Grogan said. "He won't bite. Will's a good boy, if I do say so. He may tease a bit, but I promise he won't step over the line. His ma and me, we brought him up right." He flapped his hand in a shooing motion.

Ruthy chewed on her lip as the wagons moved ahead. She certainly didn't want to encourage Will Grogan. But she did want to see that book of maps. She'd never seen one before. It wouldn't take but a few seconds. She'd just pretend he was one of her brothers, tell him what his papa said and hurry back to the front. What could he do, after all? He had to stay with his wagon and she could move around. She wouldn't have to stand there and listen to him a bit longer than she wanted to. She'd ask him.

As she waited for Will's wagon, she tried out some words in her head. *"Will, your papa said you should let me look at that book of maps."* Did that sound too much like she was ordering him around?

"Will, could I please look at that book of maps next time we stop? Your papa said it was all right with him." Maybe that sounded like she was begging. She wasn't going to beg. Not from Will Grogan.

His wagon rolled even with Ruthy. Will looked down from the perch behind his mules and grinned. "Well, well, well! Will you look at that? Company in the middle of the morning and me with my hair uncombed." He lifted his hat with a grand motion and smoothed his dark brown hair, using extra-large movements as if he were acting on a stage. "Good morning to you, fair maid."

Settling his hat back on his head, he flapped the reins unnecessarily. "To what do I owe the honor of this visit?" He continued to grin.

Ruthy frowned. "Don't flatter yourself, Will Grogan. I

didn't come to visit you. I just came to bring you a message. Your papa said I could see that book of maps at the next stop."

Will's face puckered up. He brought a hand to his chest. "I'm saddened beyond belief. I was so hoping you came back here to brighten my day."

Ruthy's expression grew fierce. She might have known he'd act a fool. "Well, I didn't. I just came to ask about the maps like your papa told me to. Now I have, and I'm going." She flounced ahead, intending to bring the entire encounter to an end.

"Wait a minute, Ruthy," Will protested. "What's your hurry? At least, stay long enough to tell me why you want to see the maps. Don't pay any attention to me. I just like to tease, don't mean anything by it."

But Ruthy didn't answer. Will Grogan always made her feel mixed up. Moving even faster and squinting at the western sun, she told herself she could do without the maps. She didn't need to see them at all if it meant putting up with that smart-aleck. If she ignored Will forever, it would be just what he deserved.

Still, she couldn't quite stop herself from stealing a quick backward glance toward the last wagon in the line.

CHAPTER 19

Damaged

The wagons pulled up a bit early that evening. The travelers could see the Ohio River, just as Perk had predicted.

"Seems to me like we ought to wait till morning afore crossing," Perk told the group. "How does that set with you?" He looked from Mr. Keeter to Mr. Grogan.

"Fine by me," Mr. Grogan said. "I'll go get some water. Will, you see to the mules. While you're at it, take care of Keeter's team too." He looked at the other man. "If you agree."

Mr. Keeter nodded and quietly set about lighting the cook fire. He used sticks he'd gathered at the noon stop. "Mrs. Perkins," he said. "I don't know what you was planning for supper, but I wonder if maybe we hadn't better use the last of that deer meat Perk brought in Wednesday. Been long enough in the back of my wagon, wouldn't surprise me none if it's near to going bad."

94

"I expect you're right," Kizzie said. She turned to Ruthy. "Could you see to that? I need to feed the baby."

Ruthy got the iron cook pot and followed Mr. Keeter.

He climbed into his wagon. "I'll cut the last good parts off the bone and hand them out to you."

"All right." Ruthy rested the pot on the end board and waited for the chunks of meat.

"Mr. Keeter," she asked, staring hard at a knot in the wood in front of her, "do you ever feel fearful for those back home?"

"Fearful? Not particularly, child. Lonesome, sometimes, but not fearful. We live near my wife's kin. They'll watch over all that's mine. Why? Do you?"

"Some," Ruthy admitted. She dropped her left arm from the pot and shook it to relieve a cramp. "Mama and Papa seem so far away. I've never been away before, you know." She brushed at a fly buzzing around the meat and blinked back tears.

"There," Mr. Keeter said. He peered into the pot. "That should pretty well do it. I'll bury the bone. Don't want the wolves smelling it. A shame we don't have a dog. He'd love to gnaw on a good bone like this"

He looked down at Ruthy's sagging shoulders. "Homesick, are you?"

She nodded.

He stepped to the ground and patted her shoulder. "Not surprising. It's natural. Don't wallow around in it, though. Try to keep your mind busy. Think about what lies ahead. A good night's sleep is a blessing, too." He patted her shoulder again and gently nudged her toward the fire. "The coals should be about ready. Better get the meat cooking." He picked up his shovel and moved off into gathering dusk.

Ruthy put the meat on to boil and added an onion they'd brought from the Patterson garden. It would be nice to have something else to go with the venison.

Baked potatoes. They hadn't had those in days. They usually just cut their potatoes in pieces and tossed them in the pot with the meat and onions. It was easier. But they had time tonight. She chose six of the largest left in the burlap bag, broke off several small sprouts, rubbed the skins with a piece of salt pork, and shoved them into the hot ash bed at the edge of the fire.

Now what?

She checked the campsite. Kizzie was still in the wagon, caring for Feelie. The stock were staked out, munching on hay and a bit of corn. She couldn't see any of the men. They must have walked down to the river to check on tomorrow's ferry. It would have been fun to go with them. Seemed like girls always had to stay behind.

The lonely feeling hiding in her chest all day grew stronger. She wondered if Mama was tending her supper fire right now, like she was. Was Papa in the barn, milking? Or had he finished? And Molly-dog? Was she well? Ruthy wished with her whole heart that she could be back home, if only for a little while. Even if they did have mush to eat. "I wouldn't complain this time," she vowed.

Heaving a deep sigh, Ruthy checked the simmering meat. A sharp, swirling breeze blew smoke into her eyes. She coughed, blinked, and moved aside.

"Hey, Ruthy-Ruth! Here's that book of maps you asked

for." It was Will Grogan, coming out of nowhere, when she thought she was alone, and calling her a stupid name like "Ruthy-Ruth." For two cents, she'd poke him with a stick. Still, he had that map book. Her fingers itched to feel its cover and turn its pages. So, pretending politeness, Ruthy wiped her hands on her skirt and held them out.

"Thank you, Will. I'll take good care of it."

Will grinned and moved the large, flat book out of her reach. "Not so fast. This is not your average book. Pa ordered it all the way from Philadelphia and probably paid a pretty piece for it. Besides, I'm not sure a girl can understand maps that well. Especially if you've never seen them before. Don't you think I'd better sit down by you and help you hold it?" He looked around. "That big rock over there looks wide enough for two."

"Will Grogan, I'm completely able to hold that book all by myself. And I can so understand maps. You think you're so smart because you're a boy. Girls have sense too. Now, give it to me. Your pa said I could look at it."

She reached up, grabbed hold of one edge of the book, and tugged hard. Just as she did, Will turned loose. It was a lot like pulling on a door just as someone pushed from the other side when you weren't expecting it. Ruthy staggered back. Her fingers slipped. The brand-new book of maps flew from her grip and sailed through the air. Both young people watched in horror as it landed on the fire, knocking the pot over and scattering coals, meat, and half-roasted potatoes every which way.

They stared at the disaster, momentarily frozen in dismay. Will moved first. He sprang to the remains of the fire and grabbed the book. Muttering something that sounded a lot like a swear word, he began swiping at the cover with his bare hands, leaving streaks every place he touched.

"Here," Ruthy said. "Let me have it. You're only making it worse." Shielding her hand in a clean corner of her apron, she took the book and brushed at the ashes and bits of meat and gravy. But it was no use. They'd rescued the book in time to save it from burning, but several large scorch marks marred the back cover and gravy stains spotted the entire front.

"Why did you have to go and grab at it like that?" Will asked.

"I wouldn't have if you'd just given it to me like you were supposed to," Ruthy snapped. "But, no; you had to try and aggravate me and now look at what you caused."

Will pulled a grubby handkerchief from his pants pocket and dabbed again at some untouched spots. "It will never sell now. When he sees this, Pa will have a fit. I wouldn't be surprised if he made me work half the rest of my natural life to pay for it."

As the two mourned the ruined book, Kizzie came from the wagon. She instantly spotted the scattered remains of supper. "The food," she shrieked. "Ruthy! Will! What are you two about? Don't just stand there. Help me." She grabbed the cooking kettle and rushed from one bit of meat to the next, picking each piece off the ground, and rubbing it on her apron.

"We'd better help," Ruthy said. She gathered her gravy-stained apron into a pouch and moved toward the nearest half-cooked potato.

Will laid the book gently on the wide rock near the fire and began to shove the remaining coals back into a pile. A few sticks placed on top soon had the fire blazing again.

"I don't know what has come over you two," Kizzie scolded. "What were you thinking?" She paused in her task of gathering up the meat and glanced toward the rock where the maps rested. "I'll just bet it had something to do with that-there book. I wish to goodness Perk had never mentioned them maps." She glared at Ruthy. "You ain't been the same since. Books have their place, I reckon, but it sure ain't around where a body is making supper."

Ruthy ducked her head. "I'm sorry, Kizzie. Really and truly." She reached for the last potato, forgetting to cover her hand with the corner of her skirt. "Ouch!" she cried. She blew on her fingers and shook them. "This one is hotter than the others."

Kizzie wasn't to be sidetracked by burnt fingers. "Sorry won't bring back supper," she said. She looked at the grimy meat in the kettle. "Better rinse this off and get it going again."

"I'll get some water." Still clutching her gathered apron in one hand, Ruthy rushed to bring the water bucket.

"Where's the onions?" she asked, peering into the kettle as Kizzie sloshed the water around the meat. "Did you pick them up?"

"They was only in bits and pieces," Kizzie said. "So I left them alone. No way could I make those little bitty things fit to eat again. Plain meat is what we'll have and be glad of it."

"And the potatoes," Ruthy reminded her. She shoved them back into the edge of the ashes. "I'm pretty sure there'll still be enough for everyone. If there isn't," she added to Kizzie's stiff back, "I'll do without."

Kizzie didn't answer.

Ruthy looked around for Will, but he'd disappeared.

Just what I would have expected, Ruthy thought. Probably hopes he won't have to 'fess up to his own foolishness. If he hadn't tried to tease me, none of this would have happened.

She picked up the book and touched it gently. Poor thing! It never asked to be treated like that. It looked terrible. No one would ever buy it now. Mr. Grogan would lose the money he had in it. And it was a lot her fault. Well, hers and Will's, but mainly hers. She'd flown off the handle again. She guessed she'd have to 'fess up, herself, as much as she hated the idea. Apologizing was so hard. Her mind jumped back to that awful day last fall at the McMinn's. At least, this time, it was only about a book, not a boy. Still, she felt like hiding in the wagon and never coming out until they got to the end of their journey. A terrible tiredness washed over her. She sank to the large rock and stared at the fire, the book in her lap and her shoulders hunched.

Not long after that, the three men came back from the river. Will trailed behind, his head hanging.

"What's this I hear about my map book?" Mr. Grogan asked. "Will tells me he made a right mish-mash of things." He turned to glare at his son.

Ruthy looked at Will in surprise. He'd already said it was his fault. He was braver than she thought. Not to be outdone, Ruthy said, "It wasn't just Will, Mr. Grogan. I shouldn't have pulled on it. But we didn't mean it. Honest."

"I'm sure that you didn't, Miss Ruthy," Mr. Grogan said. "But it happened."

Ruthy hung her head, gathered a bit of her skirt in one hand, and began to twist it. "I have a little money. Can I pay you for it?"

Mr. Grogan's laugh was harsh. "I'm not that far gone, that I'd take money off a girl child, far from home. No, I put most of the blame on Will. He's older and he should have known better. We'll just take the loss." He slashed the air with his hand. "And that's the end of it."

Turning his head, he looked toward Kizzie and softened his voice. "Mrs. Perkins, ma'am. I'm sorry for all this to-do. How much time do we have before supper?"

Kizzie checked the cook pot and poked at a potato. "About a half hour, from the looks of things. I'm sorry. We got set back a bit by all that's gone on."

"Not your fault," Mr. Grogan said. He nodded to her, put his hand to his hat brim as if to tip it and walked away, motioning to Will to follow.

No one said another thing about the damaged book of maps, still resting on the nearby stone.

I've made a mess of things again. Mr. Grogan was kind, considering what happened, but I feel so guilty. How I wish I could be home tonight! I wish I'd never had to leave! I want to be with Mama and Papa. I want to pat Molly's head and smooth her ears. I know Papa would want me to be brave so I will try. But sometimes it's very hard. I can't wait until we get to St. Genevieve so I can have a letter.

(I may have to change my mind about Will. He may turn out to be better than I thought.)

CHAPTER 20

Berry's Ferry

The small wagon train crossed the Ohio River early the next morning. Theirs were the only wagons in line. Ruthy had never seen a steam ferry before, much less crossed a river on one. She was curious and nervous at the same time. The Ohio River was wider than the ones they crossed earlier and the current moved strongly from right to left as it moved to join the Mississippi.

Kizzie was nervous too. She bundled Feelie into her cradle and spoke sharply. "Ruthy, if Perk or I tell you to do something this morning, you mind what we say that instant. Do you hear me? For once in your life, don't ask questions. And watch out for Feelie, will you? I have to hold the reins while Perk leads us onto that contraption."

"I will, Kizzie," Ruthy said. "But it's all right if I look, isn't it?" She pushed her bonnet back and peered eagerly over Kizzie's shoulder.

The ferry was tied up near the bank. A ramp ran from the front of the vessel to a bit of muddy land on the river's edge. This steamboat wasn't anywhere near as big as Ruthy had thought it would be. There was only one flat deck and a roof. Two tall smokestacks stuck up through the roof. A wooden tower with window openings on all four sides stood just behind the stacks.

Ruthy saw part of a large wheel with spokes in front of one of the tower openings. That must be where the pilot steered the boat. She wondered what it would be like to be up that high. The pilot could probably see for miles. Did they let passengers come up there and look out? She'd love to do that.

Just as she drew in her breath to ask Kizzie what she thought, Perk came back from talking to the ferryman. "Mr. Berry says he's ready for us to load. Lucky for us his rig can hold four wagons and teams at a time. We can all cross together. I'll tell the others." He started away, then paused. "Kizzie, the fee for our wagon is two dollars and a half. Two for the wagon and team and me. A quarter each for you and Ruthy. Berry didn't say nothing about the baby so I didn't ask. I ain't got but six bits in my pocket. Can you get the rest out of the pouch?"

"That's quite a lot, Perk. Ain't there any other way?" Kizzie asked.

"No, this is it. I've been expecting it all along. They know we have to get across and this is the only ferry for miles. That's why I've been so close with our savings. Get the money. I'll be back."

Kizzie wound the reins around the wagon brake,

crawled back over her seat and moved toward the rear. "Sit up where I was, Ruthy. And I'd appreciate it if you'd look forward and not turn your head. I trust you, but still and all..."

"I won't look," Ruthy said. She pulled her bonnet on again and held her head stiffly forward, but couldn't resist listening. She heard a trunk latch snap open, then a bump that sounded like Kizzie lifting the tray from inside the trunk. Several moments of soft rustling followed, then sounds of the tray being dropped back in place and the trunk latch being snapped closed.

"You can look, now," Kizzie said.

Ruthy relaxed and twisted her head from side to side, stretching her neck muscles. "I hate for you and Perk to have to pay for me." She shifted back to her original perch and let Kizzie return to the wagon seat.

"Don't worry," Kizzie said. "Your pa give us some extra, just for things like this."

Almost before Kizzie got herself set and her skirts arranged, Perk returned.

He walked to Jake, the lead horse on the left, and took hold of the bridle's cheek strap.

Kizzie knuckles were white as she held the reins. "I've never done this before," she muttered.

"You did when we got on that rope-pulled ferry," Ruthy said.

"But not on one like this," Kizzie said.

Just then, the whistle sounded. Ruthy jumped and so did the Perkins team. Jake reared up and whinnied with fear, practically lifting Perk off his feet. Jerry, the other horse, followed his partner's lead.

"Whoa, there! Whoa," Perk called. He yanked on the bridle strap. "Settle down, now." The wild-eyed horses kept snorting, jerking their heads, and sidestepping. Jerry lunged forward.

Kizzie braced her feet and pulled back on the reins.

Confused, the horses began to back up.

"Don't pull so hard on the reins, Kizz," Perk yelled. "Give them a little more slack. For Lord's sake, woman, they're scared enough without your tearing at their mouths that way. Stop yanking. I've got them."

Kizzie eased the reins a bit. "You don't have to yell. I was just trying to help. And you don't need to take the Lord's name in vain, neither!"

Perk muttered something under his breath and turned back to his team. Calming his voice, he urged both horses forward. With a final lunge, the wagon moved through the muddy ruts at the end of the ramp, up the slope and onto the boat. The movement of the horses and wagon caused the ferry's deck to bob up and down. Small waves slapped against the sides.

Ruthy stood and shoved her bonnet back again. "For a minute, there, I wasn't sure what was going to happen. I thought you did good, Kizzie. Perk shouldn't have yelled like that." She stuck her head out from under the wagon cover. This was exciting. She didn't want to miss a thing.

"Move as far to the rear left side as you can," the steamboat man directed Perk. "And keep hold of your team. I've been running this ferry for nigh onto three years and ain't

106

had nobody go over the side yet. Don't want to this time, neither."

Perk led his horses to the indicated spot. Mr. Grogan's wagon moved up to their right. Mr. Keeter pulled in behind them and Will parked behind his father.

Ruthy climbed over trunks and boxes to the back of their wagon. What would the ferryman do now? To her disappointment, Will Grogan's wagon blocked most of her view.

He grinned at her and waved. "Think you'll get seasick? Bobbing up and down on the river like this?"

Ruthy frowned at the suggestion. "Worry about yourself, Will Grogan. Not me." She turned her head and called to Kizzie. "Can I get down and watch us start?"

Kizzie didn't answer. Assuming silence meant consent, Ruthy climbed down and moved between the wagons toward the side of the ferry closest to the river bank.

The ferryman and his helper pulled the ramp onto the deck and shifted two white board fences into place to block the entrance. "There," the ferryman said. "All set."

He turned to his helper. "Is the steam up?"

"Ought to be," the helper said. "I stuck plenty of wood in the firebox and I heard the escape valve hissing awhile ago."

"Good," the ferryman said. He walked toward the ladder leading to the wheelhouse and spotted Ruthy. "Better get back in your wagon, young lady. This ain't no place for you, all by your lonesome."

"I just want to watch us move away from the bank," Ruthy said. "Then I'll go."

The ferryman grunted and began to climb. The helper walked to the rear, opened a door to a shabby room and went inside. While the door stood ajar, Ruthy could see a glow and hear the hissing of steam. The door closed, a bell rang above her head, a whistle shrieked, the big paddle-wheel behind the little room began to turn, and the water between the boat and the shore grew wider and wider.

Ruthy hugged herself in excitement. She was on a steamboat, crossing the Ohio River. When they got to the other side they wouldn't be in Kentucky any more. They'd be in Illinois, two whole states away from Tennessee. Even though there was no one left on the bank to wave to, she waved anyway.

CHAPTER 21

Third Letter Home

Southern Illinois
Oct. 16, 1837

Dear Mama and Papa,

We crossed the Ohio River on a steam ferry this morning with little trouble. One of Mr. Grogan's mules tried to
balk when getting off, but was soon persuaded of the error
of his ways.

The ferry was only one story high and, when fully
loaded, sat quite low in the water. It only took two men to
run it—the captain in the wheelhouse to steer and a mate
to engage the gears of the steam engine and make the
paddlewheel turn. You see that I have learned quite a few
new words. Mr. Keeter says, at this rate, I shall soon
sound like an old river hand.

I have some very disappointing news. Mr. Berry, the ferry owner, convinced Perk and the other men to take the lower route to the Mississippi River, instead of going up to St. Genevieve to cross. If you have sent a letter there, I won't be able to read it and I am completely sick at heart. I suppose I shall have to wait for a letter until we end our journey in Springfield.

Dear Mama and Papa, I hope you have not had any more trouble, now that I am gone. I miss you a lot.

Your loving daughter,
Ruth Ann Donohue

CHAPTER 22

An Ill-advised Visit

The excitement of crossing the Ohio soon gave way again to the daily sameness of travel. The road lead across southern Illinois through a town called "Golconda." Ruthy wondered about the strange name and asked Mr. Grogan if he knew anything about it, but he didn't and they didn't stop to ask.

The next town was Vienna. They wouldn't have stopped there either, but the evening before, Mr. Keeter noticed a big crack in his wagon's front axle as he greased the wheel sockets. The men gathered around to inspect the damage. Ruthy watched and listened from a distance.

"I'm just surprised it isn't one of mine," Mr. Grogan said. "When I think about some of the chugholes we've hit." He shook his head. "These roads certainly leave a lot to be desired."

"It has to be fixed," Perk said. "I purely hate to take the

time, but we'd be in real trouble if it broke down entirely, out aways from help."

"I'm sorry to hold us up," Mr. Keeter said.

"Ain't your fault," Perk told him. "Like Grogan said, it could have happened to any of us. We'll stop at the next town and see if someone there knows a way to repair it. Putting in a whole new axle would be costly, not to mention how much time it would take."

Ruthy hurried over to Kizzie. "Did you hear that?" she whispered. "We're going to stop at the next town. Oh, Kizzie, do you think we could visit a store? I'd like that beyond anything."

"So would I." Kizzie's eyes sparkled.

And that's what they did. The blacksmith said a couple of iron bands welded tight around the crack would do the job temporarily and he could get to it later that day. So Kizzie and Ruthy began to make plans.

Ruthy dug into her trunk and picked up her best petticoat—the one with the coins in the band. She took hold of the thread holding the smallest coin in place and started to pull. Then she stopped, Papa's warning echoing in her ears. He'd said only for emergencies.

This wasn't an emergency, exactly, but it was pretty important. Ruthy hadn't had any candy in a very long time. And it would only cost a penny—or maybe two, if she got some for Kizzie. She held the thread in her hand, struggling with her thoughts. Finally she sighed, released the thread and stuffed the petticoat down in one corner of the trunk, as deep as she could make it go. She'd better do without.

If she ever married a rich man, she thought, she'd have bowls of candy in every room. And two in the kitchen.

"You ready?" Kizzie called.

"I guess so." Ruthy climbed out of the wagon and they walked up the street.

The general store Ruthy and Kizzie visited had a little bit of everything for sale: food, tools, cloth, sewing supplies, hats ... and candy. Jars and jars of candy: peppermints, lemon drops, sugared nutmeats, chewy toffee, and strings of liquorice. Ruthy's teeth ached with wanting some. It was a good thing she hadn't brought her money with her, she thought, or she'd have had to buy some lemon drops.

It didn't help Ruthy's longings any when a woman with a hoarse voice came in at that moment and asked for a sack of peppermints. "My throat is so sore, I can't hardly swallow," the woman told the clerk. "Maybe these will help."

"And while I'm here," the woman continued, handing over some money for the candy, "what would you recommend for someone with the grippe? The way my head feels, I may be coming down with it. Always be prepared, I say."

The clerk suggested an elixir in a blue bottle and the woman gave him another coin. On her way out, the woman noticed Ruthy, still staring at the candy.

"I like your hair, child," she said. She reached out to touch Ruthy's head. "You're new in town, aren't you?"

Tearing her eyes away from the displayed sweets, Ruthy smiled. "Thank you, ma'am. I'm from the wagon train down yonder." She pointed. "My friend and I are just visiting while one of our wagons gets fixed."

Ruthy's eyes dropped to the peppermint sack. "I hope your throat feels better soon."

"That's kind of you," the woman said, politely covering her mouth as she coughed. She patted Ruthy's cheek and held out her candy sack. "Would you like a peppermint?"

"Oh, yes," Ruthy said. "I love peppermints. Thank you." She took one and popped it into her mouth.

"You're welcome, child," the woman said. "Have a safe journey." She walked out, leaving Ruthy and Kizzie to their examination of all they could buy if only they had enough money.

Two days after they left Vienna, Ruthy woke up with a headache. It got worse as the morning wore on. By the middle of the morning, her whole body hurt. Every bump in the road made her feel as if her bones were about to fall apart.

"Kizzie, I don't know what's wrong, but I feel awful."

Kizzie laid the back of her hand against Ruthy's forehead. "You're burning up with fever." She turned. "Perk, we need to hold up a bit. Ruthy's got a terrible fever and I don't know what else."

Perk pulled up at the next grove of trees and went to explain to the others.

Kizzie made Ruthy's bed in its usual spot, atop the boxes and trunks. "Bed is the best place for you. I'll make a cool compress for your head. That should help. I wish I had some willow bark for an infusion. I've heard that works on a fever, but I don't have any."

Ruthy crawled under the quilts. She couldn't ever remember feeling so bad. Not even when she had the measles all those years ago. She was vaguely aware of the cool, wet

114

cloths Kizzie laid on her head but everything else dimmed as her fever raged and her body aches got worse and worse.

The next several days were mostly one big blur. She roused from time to time to drink some water and swallow some evil-tasting concoction Kizzie hoped might help. She remembered using the chamber pot every so often but that was all.

She never knew the entire group discussed whether to stop their travels until she got better and decided to move on unless she grew worse. She never knew Will Grogan filled their bucket with fresh water every morning without being asked, and Mr. Keeter spent two hours finding some willows, so Kizzie could make an infusion from the bark.

She missed the experience of crossing the Mississippi River. She didn't see the ferry. She even missed knowing they were in the state of Missouri at last. Her whole world narrowed to hot, achy hours under the quilts in the back of a covered wagon that swayed and jolted by day and seemed to stifle her at night.

CHAPTER 23

Big Surprise

When Ruthy became fully aware of her surroundings again, she felt strangely light and cool, almost as if she were floating. The aches were gone and everything around her was quiet and still.

"Mama?" she croaked. No, that wasn't right. She tried again. "Kizzie?" Her voice didn't want to work. She cleared her throat and called louder. "Kizzie? Perk? Is anybody there?"

"I see you finally decided to come back to the land of the living." Kizzie's head appeared above the wagon's end gate. She climbed in and crouched down, laying her hand on Ruthy's forehead. "Praise be, your fever is gone at last. I just knew if I kept you covered up long enough, I'd sweat it out of you. But don't tell Mr. Keeter I'm taking credit. He'll be sure it was his willow bark infusion that did the trick."

"Whatever it was, I feel a lot better." Ruthy said.

116

"That's good. You had us plenty worried. For awhile, there, you were so sick I thought we might have to see if we could find a doctor."

Ruthy ran her tongue over her dry lips. "Could I have some water?"

She propped herself up on one elbow and sipped from the dipper Kizzie lifted from a nearby bucket.

The water felt so refreshing to Ruthy's dry mouth. She savored the feeling as it wet her lips, flowed over her tongue and trickled down her throat. She took a second, larger swallow. Even better.

"Better not take too much at once," Kizzie said. She moved the dipper away. "You can have some more after awhile."

Ruthy laid her head down and wiped the back of her hand across her mouth. Strange. Even her arm felt weak. "Where are we?" she asked. "Have we gotten to the Mississippi River yet?"

Kizzie chuckled. "That, right there, shows how bad off you've been. I was pretty sure you didn't know much of what was going on. We crossed the Mississippi two days ago. We're in Missouri now—passed Jackson yesterday."

"I missed it entirely?" Ruthy propped herself up on one elbow. "What was it like, Kizz? Was it really as wide as everybody says? Shoot fire! I wanted to see the Mississippi."

"Yeah, it was as wide as you heard, maybe wider. If I didn't know better, I'd say most all the water in the whole wide world had come together, just to make that one river," Kizzie said. "I kept wondering what we'd do, if our ferry broke down right in the middle, but it didn't. It wasn't a steam ferry, though. They ran it with horses on a treadmill. Pore things. Their whole life, all they do is go round and round, never getting nowhere."

"I wonder how come they didn't have a steam engine," Ruthy said.

"I don't know. I did see a steamboat going up river but there wasn't none to carry us across. Just the horses on the treadmill."

"What about the last town we passed through? Did you say 'Jackson'?"

"Yeah. What about it?"

"Was it very big? What did it look like?" Ruthy asked.

"I didn't see very much. I heard Feelie squalling and you threw your covers off just as we went through, so I had a lot on my mind. The only thing I saw was a big rock house." Kizzie rubbed the back of her neck and turned her head from side to side as she did so. "You know, I wonder what it's like, to live in a rock house. Do you suppose it's cool all the time, like a cave? I've never lived in any kind of house but one made of logs."

"They had rock houses back in Hawkins County. I was only in one that I remember, but they were just about like all the others, I think."

Sitting back on her heels, Kizzie scrubbed at her eyes with her knuckles and blinked. "I hope I'm not taking what you've had," she said. "Ever since yesterday, I've been feeling like the wagon run over me. Is that how you felt?

"Oh, don't worry," she continued, seeing the expression of alarm on Ruthy's face. "I won't get real sick. Can't afford to, with all I have to do. I'm probably just tired." She straightened her shoulders. "I'd better check on Feelie and get supper started. She's been riding in Mr. Keeter's wagon since you come down with the fever. An old granny woman back home, she thought people might catch sicknesses from other people, so I thought . . ." Kizzie shook her head. "Probably a foolish idea. Everybody knows it's the night air. Still—better safe than sorry, I always say."

Kizzie moved to climb down. "Need anything else right now?"

"Just more rest," Ruthy said. "I feel as weak as one of Molly's newborn pups."

"Well, if you need anything, just call. One of us will hear."

Kizzie disappeared. Ruthy nestled deeper into her quilts, hoping to get back her strength. She didn't like being so weak.

Next morning, Ruthy felt even better. She crawled from under her covers, intending to get up and go outside. As she struggled to her feet, a wave of dizziness rushed through her head. Staggering, she grabbed onto one of the hoops holding up the wagon canvas. For several long minutes, she felt as if the entire wagon was whirling round and round, with her at the center. When it stopped and her head cleared, she eased back to a sitting position. Maybe she wouldn't leave the wagon after all. She'd sit up, instead, and rest her back.

At noon, Mr. Grogan came to see her. "It's nice to see you're feeling better, Miss Ruthy. I brought you a gift to help pass the time." He handed Ruthy the big book of maps.

"It isn't much of a gift. Somebody or other . . ." His

mouth crooked in a twisted smile. "Of course, the cover isn't all it used to be. But the inside pages are fine."

Ruthy looked at the title, *Tanner's Universal Atlas*. She smoothed her hand over the brown cover, stopping at one of the charred spots. "The book of maps! Oh, Mr. Grogan, I wondered what happened to it. The last I remember, it was lying on the rocks." She looked up. "Are you sure?"

At Mr. Grogan's nod, she opened it at random and read, "The State of Illinois." The outlined state was full of light colored areas and small printed words connected by lines. She turned the page with care. "The State of Indiana" came next. Ruthy looked up again, her face beaming with joy. "Are you sure you're sure?" she asked again. "The inside pages aren't a bit dirty. If you didn't see the cover, you wouldn't know anything happened at all. Couldn't you put some paper over the front or something and still sell it?"

"I might," Mr. Grogan said. "But I'm not. The book is yours. I hope it pleasures you." With that, he raised a hand and walked away

Ruthy covered her mouth in astonishment. A book of all the maps in the entire country … She'd never had any thought of having a book like this. She felt like running and shouting, even if she didn't have the strength. For sure, she couldn't sit still. She clapped her hands and wished she felt like bouncing.

Counting those in the trunk, she, Ruth Ann Donohue, only twelve years old but going on thirteen, now owned three books—all by herself. Glory, hallelujah! Getting sick was almost worth it, if it brought things like this. Maybe, if she married that rich man, she'd have a roomful of books as well as all the bowls of candy.

Oct. 24, 1837

I want to remember how it feels to be really sick. Someday, I may have to take care of someone, myself. Cool compresses are good. So are kind words, warm broth, and fresh water. I will also put the willow bark infusion receipt in my Housewife Book. I'm pretty sure it helped, even if the taste was awfully vile.

I'll not write home about being sick. Mama and Papa would just worry. I don't think it's deceiving them—not exactly—just leaving out something they can't do anything about.

CHAPTER 24

Collapse

Ruthy studied the map book, off and on. all that day, between naps. She learned why it was called an atlas. Mr. Grogan said the name was from a Greek tale about a man named Atlas, who held the sky on his shoulders. Which he didn't, of course, but it made a good story. She decided that different colors were for different counties and the words in small print were names of towns. She figured out which lines were rivers, county boundaries, and roads.

She spent a lot of time looking at her home state of Tennessee. She found Hawkins County, where Papa and Mama were, and Rogersville, the county seat where she had to go to court last summer. Somehow, looking at a map of her own county made her feel closer to home. She touched her fingers to her lips and laid them gently on that spot on the page.

Just after lunch, Ruthy heard cries of alarm. Curious, she lifted the wagon cover a few inches to see what was wrong.

Kizzie lay on the ground in a heap, not far from the noon cook fire. Perk knelt beside her. "Kizzie, what's wrong?" he called. No answer. Perk gave his wife a small shake. "Kizzie, can you hear me?"

The other men stood near, looking anxious, hands hanging loosely at their sides.

What was wrong with Kizzie? Had she stumbled over something and fallen down? Why didn't she answer when Perk called? Should she, Ruthy, leave the wagon and try to help?

It was a relief when Kizzie began to stir. With Perk's help, she sat up. She said something, but her voice was too weak for Ruthy to hear.

When Kizzie moved, so did all the others. "She needs to lie down, Perkins," Mr. Grogan said.

"Can I do something to help?" Will asked. "Could you use some water?" He grabbed the water bucket and ran toward the stream.

Mr. Keeter didn't say anything. He just nodded to Perk, reached down, and put his hands under one of Kizzie's arms. He and Perk helped her stand and, together, they struggled toward the wagon.

Ruthy realized she needed to get up. There really wouldn't be room for two beds under the canvas. Grabbing the top quilt, she wrapped it around her so the men wouldn't have to see her standing in her nightgown, and struggled to her feet. She was still a bit dizzy but nothing like last time.

"Ruthy," Perk called. "We need to get Kizzie into the wagon. Are you decent?"

"I'm up," Ruthy said. She stuck her head out the back. "Let me get down, first."

She took Mr. Keeter's hand and clambered out. It wasn't easy to hold the quilt around her and get out at the same time, but she did her best.

"What's wrong with Kizz?" she asked.

"I don't know," Perk said. "She just up and collapsed, right while she was stirring the beans. She's lucky she didn't land in the fire."

Remembering what Kizzie had done when she felt bad, Ruthy stuck one hand out and felt her friend's forehead.

"Why, she's burning up," Ruthy said, unconsciously echoing the older woman.

"She told me this morning she didn't feel good, but I didn't think she felt this bad."

"I only need to rest awhile," Kizzie muttered. "Just let me have a little lie down. I'll be all right in a bit."

Perk and Mr. Keeter helped Kizzie into the cocoon of blankets so recently vacated. Perk gave her a small sip of water. Ruthy watched carefully. Will and his father hovered near.

"The baby's crying her head off," Will said. "Should I get her?" He sounded uncertain.

"I will," Mr. Keeter said as he stepped down from the wagon bed. He looked back at Ruthy. "She's been riding in my wagon while you was sick, but her ma still had the care of her. I expect she needs dry linen and it wouldn't be fitten for me to do anything about that, her being a girl child like she is. It's up to you to take care of it, I guess." He looked back at Perk, still kneeling beside Kizzie. "If you agree, Perkins."

Perk adjusted the covers around Kizzie's shoulders and nodded without even looking up.

Ruthy smiled. Here was something she definitely could do to help. She'd learned a lot about babies since they left Hawkins County. "Bring her here," she said. "Then you men go away and let me get dressed. I can't take care of Kizzie and Feelie and hold this quilt around me at the same time."

"What about our nooning?" Will asked.

"Will!" Mr. Grogan said. "Is that all you ever think about—your stomach?"

"No, it ain't," Will said, "but right now I'm thinking about it. I can't stop being hungry because Kizzie's got a fever."

"You and me can see to the food," Mr. Keeter said, "soon as I get the babe and her cradle moved in beside her ma. I ain't much of a hand to cook, but I'll bet, between us, we can make shift to dish up what Mrs. Perkins was working on."

Somehow it all got done. They moved a couple of boxes to make room for Feelie's cradle and Ruthy got the small child changed and settled. She had a fleeting thought about whether the baby was likely to get sick, lying so near her mother, but forgot it in all the bustle. Mr. Grogan brought Ruthy's food to the wagon. Kizzie roused long enough to nurse Feelie but said she didn't feel like eating a bite, herself. She took another sip of water and lay with her eyes closed.

Ruthy leaned against a wooden box, a quilt wrapped around her for warmth, and watched Kizzie's face, looking for the slightest change. Thank goodness, Feelie had gone to sleep after she ate. Ruthy was beginning to feel drowsy, herself, when footsteps crunched outside.

"I brung some more willow-bark water." It was Mr. Keeter. "I figure if it helped you, it ought to help her, too." He nodded toward Kizzie. "I'll make some more before we move on."

"We aren't going to stay here for a day or so?" Ruthy asked. "I know we didn't stop before, but I thought, with nobody but me to do for Kizzie and the baby ..." Her voice trailed off.

"It's real dark in the northwest. This part of the country has bad storms. A big one could make the creeks get up to flood real quick. Perk thinks we ought to get as far as we can 'fore it all begins," Mr. Keeter said.

The wagons pushed on through the short afternoon. Looming clouds darkened. Powerful gusts of wind shook the wagons. Lightning sliced through the sky and thunder beat on their ears. Sometime in mid-afternoon, torrents of water began pounding the earth. The travelers could hardly see. Perk, hat pulled low, slowed his team to a crawl as he struggled to stay on the rough track substituting for a road.

Ruthy stayed busy trying to catch the leaks as the downpour worked its way through the canvas wagon top. In between times, she replaced the cool rag on Kizzie's forehead and tried her best to sooth Feelie. The child's face was flushed and she turned her head from side to side, refusing to accept the sweet sop Ruthy offered. With each thunder crash, Feelie screamed a little louder.

Her child's fearful cries finally roused Kizzie. "She's not used to this kind of noise," Kizzie said in a weak voice.

"Hand her here, will you? I'll take her in with me for awhile. Let's hope she's not getting sick, too."

Ruthy lifted the baby from her cradle and laid her cheek against Feelie's, imitating Kizzie's way of checking the child for fever. Feelie's cheek felt hot. "Her face feels feverish," Ruthy said. "You should probably check, too, to make sure. I've never done this before."

"It wouldn't do no good," Kizzie said. "My face is as hot as hers. I couldn't tell."

Ruthy laid the baby down beside Kizzie and it seemed to help them both relax. Eventually, the heaviest part of the storm blew over and, even though the rain kept falling and the canvas cover leaked, a relative calm filled the lead wagon.

CHAPTER 25

Wet Camp

Dusk came early. The drizzle, along with a cold, damp wind, made everyone miserable. They found an abandoned lean-to not far off the track, built by some settler who'd evidently given up and left. The four wagons pulled up near it and began making ready for the night.

"Anybody in here turned into a frog, yet?" It was Mr. Keeter, bringing more willow-bark tea.

"Not exactly," Ruthy said. "The rain completely soaked the canvas though. I put pans under the biggest drips. The thing is—I'm afraid the baby's sickening, too."

"Well, young lady, looks like you've got your hands full, with two sick at the same time. Do you need to get out and stretch your legs? I'll stand here and keep watch if you do. I can hand around the tea. It's left over from noon and it's cold, but I reckon it will do."

Gratefully, Ruthy rose, threw a shawl over her head as a

rain shield, and left the wagon, hobbling over the wet ground on stiff legs.

Will met her as she moved toward the dripping trees, his coat covering an armload of fallen sticks and small limbs. "Hail, fair maiden. Why hobblest thou on wobbly legs?"

"Don't "fair maiden" me, Will Grogan. Your legs would be stiff too, if you'd had to sit with a sick woman and a screaming baby all afternoon. I didn't notice you offering to take a turn."

Will dropped his teasing tone. "I couldn't. I had to drive a wagon. Besides, I don't know how to take care of sick folks. That's women's work. Men don't know about things like that, lessen they're doctors."

"Mr. Keeter does. And you could learn. That's what I'm having to do," Ruthy said.

Will's face softened. "Has Feelie really come down with it, too?"

"Her face is awfully hot. That's all I know right now, but I'm fearful."

"Will," Mr. Grogan called. "I'd truly like to get this fire started in time, at least, for breakfast tomorrow. I believe I could do it, if you'd bring me that wood."

"Coming," Will called. "Sorry," he told Ruthy.

Ruthy went back to her patients, freeing Mr. Keeter to help with supper.

This time, Perk brought the food, but Kizzie still didn't feel as if she could swallow. She did, however, drink some meat broth and water.

Ruthy looked at her own bowl with suspicion. The tough, under-cooked meat and nearly-burned corn pone didn't taste any better than it looked. The meat definitely needed a bit more time on the fire and more salt would have helped. But Ruthy ate most of it anyway. Beggars can't be choosers, she thought. Mothers ought to teach boys how to cook. I can help outside. Why couldn't they learn to help with house chores?

Supper over, Mr. Keeter appeared once more. "We have that lean-to, over there. It leaks a bit but the ground inside is mostly dry. You women can stay in it if you like. I'm not sure which will be warmer, though, the wagon or the lean-to. What do you think, Miss Ruthy? Stay or move to the shelter?"

Ruthy didn't know. Why were they asking her? They were the grownups. She wasn't. Why didn't someone simply decide and tell her? It wasn't fair. But she couldn't say that to Mr. Keeter. He obviously thought she knew enough to choose.

She looked at Kizzie and the baby. She'd just gotten them settled for the night. Moving would stir things up all over again. When she was sick, she wouldn't have wanted to have to move around. She made up her mind.

"I think we'll stay here," Ruthy said. She yawned and frowned. "But, Mr. Keeter, where should I sleep? Kizzie's in my bed and there isn't room to make down another one."

Mr. Keeter's eyes roamed over the inside of the wagon. "Got yourself a problem, all right." He pushed his hat back and scratched his head. "I guess this is all a part of you having to act growed up before you're ready. Many a time, I've seed my wife sit up in the rocking chair all night, when there was sick folk to tend. Reckon you'll have to stay right there where you're setting."

He tugged his hat back down with a jerk. "Tell you

what. I have an extra blanket and a quilt I ain't using. I'll bring them over. That wet wind is likely to feel cruel cold before morning. You can set on one and wrap up real tight in the other.

"Won't help none to feel sorry for you. I am sorry, though, that my own woman ain't along. She's real good at helping when they's sick folk around. But there . . . she's not here and we'll have to make the best of it."

He walked away, returning with two warm coverlets. Ruthy soon made a cozy nest for herself and was almost settled when Perk stuck his head through the wagon cover's back opening.

"How is she?" he asked in a hoarse whisper.

Ruthy reached out and felt Kizzie's forehead. "Feels like she's about the same. She's asleep. That's good."

Perk shook his head over and over. "I've never known Kizzie to be really sick. You don't think she's like to die, do you?" His eyes looked moist. "I don't know what I'd do without her. She can't die."

"Well, I didn't die," Ruthy said. "Even though I felt really bad for awhile. And if I didn't, why would she? Go to bed," she added. "And don't worry. My mama always says worry never solves a thing."

"It's hard not to. You'll let me know if you need anything?" Perk asked. "I'll be right here under the wagon, and I'll hear, real easy, if you call."

"I will," Ruthy said. She made herself smile, even as her mouth began to open in a big yawn. "It will be all right. You'll see. She's had two doses of Mr. Keeter's willow-bark infusion. That's bound to help."

131

"I'll be right below," Perk said again. He drew the wagon cover together as tight as he could to keep out the cold air and Ruthy began what she feared would be a very long night watch.

CHAPTER 26

Rained Out

It rained all that night and all the next day. Every creek and river flowed out of its banks, making travel impossible. A cold wind hammered the drops against the earth. The fallen leaves of autumn soaked up the water and made a sodden mass under every tree. The horses and mules huddled together for warmth as they faced away from the storm.

Ruthy struggled to keep herself, Kizzie and the baby reasonably dry, warm, and cared for. She put Feelie's wet clouts on a rope tied across the inside of the lean-to, with little hope that they would get dry even with a fire burning under the overhang all day long. She wrapped a petticoat around a hot rock and put it close to Kizzie's feet, and emptied the drip pans over and over.

Perk slogged through the mud, hunting for fresh meat, and came back with a small deer. Mr. Grogan and Mr. Keeter spent almost all day chopping fallen trees into enough logs to keep the fire burning and stacking them under the lean-to, out of the worst of the rain. Will tended the fire, constantly poking at the wet wood to urge it into flame, and turning the roasting leg of venison intended for their evening meal.

"This meat is going to be more smoked than roasted," he told Ruthy as she checked on Feelie's drying diaper cloths. "Wood this wet just won't burn hot enough to do much roasting."

It was a welcome relief when the meat finally seemed done enough to eat. Everyone, except Kizzie and Feelie, gathered for a supper of smoked, partly-roasted venison. The men took off their shoes and stuck their feet close to the fire to warm their toes and dry their socks. To Ruthy, the mixed-up smell of wet woolen socks, cooked meat, and wood smoke felt strangely homelike and cozy.

"All we need now," Perk said, "is for an early freeze to bring sleet. That would really put icing on the cake. At this rate, we could be here till spring."

Mr. Keeter leaned sideways from his place by the fire and peered at the sky. "It wouldn't surprise me none if it stopped soon. Seems to be letting up."

"Do you think we can go on tomorrow?" Will asked.

"Not likely," Mr. Keeter said. "Even if it stops, the creeks will still be too high for safe crossing."

"Not to mention mud deep enough to swallow our horses," Perk said with a sigh. He turned to Ruthy. "Kizzie told me she's feeling better. And she thinks the baby is, too. That right?"

"All I know is what she tells me," Ruthy said. "But her forehead did seem cooler last time I checked. And Feelie ate good tonight. Maybe we're past the worst of it. I sure hope so."

"As do we all," Mr. Grogan said. He stretched his arms above his head and yawned loudly.

The men planned to sleep in the lean-to and soon began to spread their blankets among the stacks of drying wood. Ruthy went back to the wagon and checked on her two patients. Nothing had changed. She wasn't quite ready to settle for the night, so she got out her pen, ink, and journal. To her disappointment, though, the paper was so damp the ink ran and her letters blurred. She sighed and put it all away. Last night had gone more quickly than she'd expected. Taking care of two sick people at once kept a person busy. Now they were better, though, time moved as slow for Ruthy as a fly crawling through spilled honey.

Kizzie lay with her eyes closed most of the time, even when she was awake. Feelie fussed for a spell, then soon went back to sleep.

Ruthy wished she could go to sleep that easily, but she felt wide awake. The cozy feeling from under the lean-to had completely evaporated. She huddled under her quilts and thought about what she'd be doing if she were back home. Probably sitting by the fire in the kitchen, working on her sampler while Papa mended harness and Mama read something aloud for all of them to enjoy. Maybe they would pop some corn. Whatever they did, it would be dry and warm and comfortable. Not cramped and cold and damp, with nothing to do. How long, she wondered, would she have to stay in Missouri? With a little luck, if all went well, maybe she could go home again by summer.

"Is anybody awake in here?" Will's voice whispered, just outside the wagon.

Ruthy glanced toward Kizzie. Her eyes were closed. "Tell him to come in, if he wants to." Kizzie murmured. "I ain't asleep."

Ruthy untied the opening in the wagon cover. Will stood, water dripping off his hat brim, holding a lantern with one hand and clutching a book under his coat with the other. " Were you all about to go to sleep?" he asked.

"No," Ruthy said. "I thought Kizzie was, but she's awake and says to come in."

Will handed his lantern to Ruthy, climbed over the end board, took off his muddy boots, and re-tied the canvas. "I'm not ready to lie down yet and thought you folks might like a little company." He looked at Kizzie. "I brought a book to share if you feel like listening."

"I'd be glad to hear it," Kizzie said. "Lying here is getting to be tedious but I don't feel like doing anything else." She looked at Will's book. "What is it?"

The Last of the Mohicans, Will said. "It's my very favorite book. Full of adventure. I've read it three times already, but I don't mind going at it again."

Kizzie closed her eyes. "I'm listening," she said. "Read as much as you've a mind to."

Will moved the lantern closer, opened the brown leather cover and began to read: "*The Last of the Mohicans: A Narrative of 1757 by James Fenimore Cooper.*" He turned the page: "*Chapter 1. It was a feature peculiar to the colonial wars of North America, that the toils and dangers of the wilderness were to be encountered before the adverse hosts could meet.*"

"That sounds like us," Ruthy said. "Toils and dangers of the wilderness."

"Lots worse than us," Will said. "Wait till you hear what happens. There's this man named Hawkeye, see, and ..."

"Don't tell us ahead of time," Ruthy said. "Read."

So he did. As the story unraveled, the world of Hawkeye's wilderness adventures filled the wagon, and the sound of Will's voice was all that mattered.

CHAPTER 27

Night Alarm

Sometime late that night, Ruthy was startled awake by a panicked voice yelling, "Help! Perk. Ruthy. Somebody help! Feelie, what's wrong? Please, Baby, don't do that!"

Ruthy bolted upright in her bed. For a fleeting moment, she thought Will was still reading an adventure from *The Last of the Mohicans*. Then she knew it was Kizzie and, from the terror in her voice, something was unbelievably wrong.

The rain had stopped and the light of a full moon managed to creep between the shifting clouds, enough so that Ruthy could see most things without a lantern. Perk, also startled by the fear in Kizzie's call, scrambled into the wagon with bare, muddy feet, clad only in his long underwear. "What's wrong? What's going on? Kizzie?"

He crawled across Ruthy's bed to Kizzie's side. Ruthy floundered over a box to make room. Kizzie knelt on her covers, clutching Feelie to her chest. The three watched in horror as the baby, body stiff and eyes rolled back into her head, jerked and twitched. Her face was red and every breath she took sounded as if she had to work hard, just to draw it in and push it out.

To Ruthy, Feelie's attack looked horrible and it seemed to go on and on. Later, though, she realized it stopped only a short time after Perk got there. As suddenly as it began, Feelie's body relaxed, her head rolled to one side, and she dropped into a sound sleep.

Perk reached out one finger, nail black with dirt, and touched his child's cheek. "She feels hot," he said in a hushed voice. "Doesn't she feel hot to you, Kizzie?"

Kizzie nodded, her face still full of fear.

"Did Feelie have a fit? Was that what it was?" Ruthy asked. "I don't understand. I thought she was getting better. Her face is awful red. What happened?"

Kizzie stroked Feelie's forehead, pushing the little girl's hair back. "All I know is, I woke up with her shaking and jerking and her eyes turned up like that and I just grabbed her and yelled." She twitched the corner of Feelie's cover. "Her face was cool when she went to sleep."

"Do you think it could happen again?" Ruthy asked.

"It certainly might, if she stays as hot as she is right now." Kizzie touched Feelie's forehead again. "She's not sweating at all. This fever is burning her up. I've never known her to be so hot."

By this time, the other men had gathered just outside.

"Got a problem in there?" Mr. Grogan called. "Can we do anything?"

Perk turned toward the back of the wagon. "The baby had a fit, we think," he answered. "And she's burning up—hotter than before." Perk turned back to Kizzie. "What do you want us to do?

Kizzie raised her shoulders and shook her head in puzzlement.

"There's got to be something we can try," Perk said. His voice sounded ragged and uneven. "I remember when I was a young'un. Ma lost the two that came after me and Polly. They was so little. We thought they only had the croup. Then it got worse and they just up and died, right there before our eyes."

"Both of them?" Ruthy asked, thinking of Perk as a small boy, maybe standing in a corner of the room, watching the children die. "You must have been awfully scared. I would have been."

"I was," Perk said. He laid his hand on Feelie's arm and stroked it. "I'll never forget it. Never. Billy died first, then, near morning, Gert went, too. We done everything we knew how, but none of it did any good. Mostly, I remember Pa crying. I never saw him do that, before or after. He was a grown man, and he just broke down and cried like a baby."

Perk wriggled his shoulders and stretched his neck as if to shake off his memories. "Maybe this time, I should look for a doctor. I'm pretty sure I could get through on Star."

Kizzie shook her head. "No. I need you here. Who knows how far you'd have to go? And it could be all for naught. And what would I do, if worse came to worst and you wasn't here?"

She sat back on her heels and stared at Feelie, biting her

lower lip. "My ma always bathed us with cold wet rags when we had a fever, but I don't remember any of us ever being this hot.

"Ruthy, you feel her," Kizzie said. "Was she this hot while I was at my sickest and didn't know much of what was happening?"

Ruthy laid her hand on Feelie's cheek. "No, she wasn't. At least, I'm pretty sure she wasn't. She's even hotter than our old dog, Mollie, was when she got hurt. Mollie cooled off in the mud."

"Well, we got plenty of that, right enough." Kizzie said, "but I hate to use mud on a baby. Mud's something pigs lie in." She bit her lip and looked at Ruthy. "Maybe I ought to try to sweat it out of her."

"But she's so hot already," Ruthy said. "Doesn't seem right to make her hotter."

"It worked for you," Kizzie reminded her.

Ruthy looked at the sick baby. She'd held her, rocked her to sleep, and changed her dirty diaper cloths. Feelie just couldn't die.

"What about putting cool mud on her?" Ruthy asked. "It worked for Molly. It might be worth a try. Goodness knows, we have plenty of water to wash it off if it doesn't."

Kizzie still hesitated.

Ruthy kept talking, afraid Kizzie's lip would start bleeding if she didn't stop biting on it soon. "I wish we had some ice but we don't. I know! Maybe we could try the cold creek water. How about that? Like your ma used to do. Only let's not just wash her with wet rags. Let's dip her right down in it, sort of like a baptizing. Remember how cold the baptizing water felt? And that was in the summer. It's bound to be a lot colder now that winter's nearly here. If that doesn't work, we could still try the mud."

Kizzie's face cleared. She stopped biting on her lip. "That's what we'll do," she said.

"Which?" Ruthy asked, just to be sure. "Mud or creek water?"

"Creek water," Kizzie said. She looked at Perk, her voice filled with new energy. "Shift these boxes over there." She pointed to the boxes near her feet and jerked her head toward the front of the wagon. "That will give us enough room to set the wash tub right here." She indicated a spot near her feet. "When you're done with that, go get the coldest creek water you can find. If there's a good, flowing spring, get some of that."

Kizzie's eyes suddenly focused sharply on her husband. "And, for pity's sake, Jimmy Perkins, put your pants on. For shame! In your underwear, in front of Ruthy." She clicked her tongue.

As Kizzie directed, Perk hurried to put his pants on, shift the boxes, and get the tub. All the men grabbed buckets and rushed to fill them with fresh creek water. Each, in turn, handed his bucket to Ruthy, who dumped it in the tub, only calling a halt when it was nearly full.

Meanwhile, Kizzie laid Feelie down and took off all her clothes, even her diaper cloth. "Nobody's here but us girls," she told Ruthy. "If anybody else comes in, I'll cover her up."

Ruthy watched as Kizzie lowered Feelie's small body into the cold water up to her chin and held her there. Feelie screamed, shocked by the cold water. She kicked and flailed her arms, splashing water everywhere. Kizzie tried to sooth her with words but held the small body firmly where it was.

"Is it working?" Perk called from outside.

"Too soon to tell," Kizzie called back. "We've got to keep the water fresh and cold, though. Let's empty this lot and get some more."

Perk climbed back in. Together, he and Ruthy lifted the water-filled tub over the surrounding boxes and quilts, heaved it onto the end-gate, and dumped it out onto the ground.

They repeated the entire procedure three more times before Kizzie said it was enough.

"Did it work?" Ruthy asked. "Is Feelie cooler?" She crawled back to Kizzie's side. "At least she's awake. That's something. Is she crying because she's cold or because she feels bad?"

"A bit of both, probably. But she seems cooler and that's a blessing," Kizzie said. Her mouth twisted in a half smile. "All we can do now is to pray the Good Lord to carry us through and ask for healing." She reached out with one arm and gave Ruthy an awkward hug. "Now, you go lay down. You've done a woman's work the last few days, and I'm grateful. But you're still a growing girl and you need your sleep. I'll take it from here."

CHAPTER 28

Pushing Through

As Mr. Keeter hoped, next day the weather changed. Ruthy slept late after the night's alarm and, by the time she woke up, the sun had come out. A constant, soft plop-plop sounded as the last drops of moisture fell from the bare branches and remaining leaves of the forest. The air felt fresh and cool. Ruthy's shoes left oozing prints when she slogged across the softened ground. Steam rose from the horses' and mules' backs as they warmed themselves in an open, sunny spot.

The day progressed much like the one before, except that Ruthy took over the cooking. Each person stopped by the wagon several times, in order to check on Feelie. When her fever didn't climb again, a general air of lightheartedness spread through the small clearing.

Will swished a stick at every low-hanging branch he encountered, sending showers of droplets flying. The horses frisked around as the sun warmed their backs. To Ruthy's amusement, Mr. Keeter sang ten verses of *Yankee Doodle* while he trimmed branches off the firewood.

Perk looked at the sunny sky and remarked to no one in particular. "I'm hoping for a clear sky tonight and a good, stiff wind to dry things out. Give me half a chance and we'll get moving again."

He strode over and looked in on Kizzie and Feelie. "Hey, there, Old Woman," he said. "You and Feelie better get well soon, so you can enjoy the view when we come into Springfield. I aim to get us there in the next few days, no matter if I have to push this wagon through the mud every step of the way. Then," he continued, "if my baby has an-other fit, there'll at least be somebody or 'other who knows more about doctoring than we do."

"Hey, yourself, Old Man," Kizzie said. "I am well. Can't you see how peart I look today? I even combed my hair." She smiled and patted her head. "Springfield sounds like heaven. How much longer, do you reckon?"

Perk began to figure aloud, bending down one finger at a time. "Let's see. If the weather holds and, say, we average at least ten to twelve miles a day, maybe a little more … counting river crossings, and if nothing else holds us up, we should pull into Springfield in fifteen or so days."

"Only a little more than two weeks. That sounds mighty fine. It will be nice to stop traveling. I have to admit, living out of this wagon is getting tiresome."

"It won't be too long," Perk said as he walked away.

Freed from nursing duties, Ruthy felt as if someone had lifted a heavy pack from her back. She took the opportunity, while watching over the noon venison stew, to write in her "Housewife's Hints" about caring for a fever victim.

That night, just as Perk had hoped, the sky was clear. The stars sparkled and seemed so close Ruthy felt as if she could almost reach out and gather them in her apron.

Perk got the wagons moving soon after first light the next morning, but the muddy ground made for slow travel. Mud clung to the wagon wheels, and the horses slipped as they struggled for footing on the slick ground. But Perk was determined to keep on going. When a wagon bogged down, he expected everyone but Kizzie and Feelie to help push and pry it out. The men hitched and unhitched the teams, adding extra animals to help pull a particular wagon, when necessary. They laid brush and limbs on top of the worst sections to give the wheels a little more traction.

Creeks and rivers were still above flood stage. Twice, they had to search up and downstream for safer places to cross. By mid-afternoon, the entire party was exhausted and covered from head to toe in mud. Still Perk urged them on.

"I've had just about enough of this," Kizzie muttered under her breath as they reached another river. She raised her voice. "James Madison Perkins," she called. "You stop this wagon right now."

Perk pulled on the reins. He took off his hat and swiped his face on his upper arm, leaving mud streaked across his cheeks. His hatband had plastered his hair to his forehead. "What's wrong? Has Feelie taken a turn again?"

"No, she hasn't," Kizzie said. "But she could, at the rate we're going. You've got to stop driving us so hard. Let's find a place to stop. We need to rest. Ask the others. They'll tell you I'm right."

Perk looked at the river ahead and at the sky with daylight still left in it. He looked at the horses, their heads drooping, mud caked all the way to their bellies, their backs dark with sweat. He frowned and his shoulders slumped. "If you're going to raise Cain, I'll check with the others. I just did it so we could get Feelie to a town with doctors and such."

"Well," Kizzie said, "I figured that out. But it won't do us no good to get the baby to town if the rest of us collapse in the process. You can't help it if the going is so hard, but you can trim your sail to fit the wind."

Ruthy wasn't clear on what "trimming the sail" meant but she crossed her fingers, hoping Mr. Keeter and Mr. Grogan were as sick of the mud as she was. She'd had to get out three or four times to help push. Her stockings were filthy and uncomfortably wet. Her soggy shoes sat side by side on a rag so she wouldn't dirty up the inside of the wagon. They might never be clean again. They might even fall apart without the mud to hold them together.

To everyone's relief, Perk said they'd stop as soon as they forded the river. "I always like to be on the far side of any water before stopping," he said.

The river bottom on the far side was just as soft as what they'd come through already. No matter where they stepped, their feet sank into the mud. In some places, it was so sticky it built up like extra soles on the bottoms of their shoes and boots. It clung until it was so thick a footprint-shaped clod would drop off in one whole piece and lie there, looking like someone had lost the entire bottom of a boot.

"We can't stop here, Kizzie," Perk said. "You can see that. I promise, we'll stop as soon as we find a decent place to camp."

True to his word, when they reached higher ground, he pulled over and stopped. The rest of the train followed his lead and made camp.

Ruthy consulted Kizzie and set about assembling a quick supper of cold venison and hastily-baked cornpone. After supper, everyone lingered around the fire. For once, all hands were still. No one seemed to have the energy even to whittle a stick.

Will stretched, shrugged his tired shoulders, and heaved a loud sigh. "To think we could have waited till spring. Warm weather, green grass." He looked at his father. "How is it again that we came this late in the year?"

"You know good and well why," Mr. Grogan said. "Perk and Keeter were going to the same place we were. I didn't want to risk the possibility of having to go it alone, next spring. Two wagons, loaded with store goods like they are, would be a real temptation to someone with more gunpowder than sense. I figured there was safety in numbers." He spat into the glowing coals.

"How come you didn't wait till spring, Mr. Keeter?" Will asked.

"That's an easy one," Mr. Keeter answered. "I sold my crops and had some hard cash. If I'd waited for spring, a lot of it—huh! most of it—would have been gone. Just wait till you have a wife and kids. They always need something. I couldn't afford to wait."

Perk took no part in the conversation. "We could have kept going," he grumbled, raking the side of his boot with a stick. No one answered him. They just rested their arms on their knees and stared at the fire.

RUTHY'S JOURNAL

November ??

It's been a long while since I've written anything. Such a time we've had! I've lost track of the days. All the sickness, and then the rain and mud and Perk pushing so hard. But it seems like we've turned the corner at last. The road, such as it is, is passable again. The creeks and rivers are back in their banks. Kizzie is well and getting stronger every day and Baby Feelie seems more like her old self—thinner than she was, but better. No more fits, for which we're all thankful.

Everything we have is covered in dried mud. We tried to keep it out of the wagon, but with it on our clothes, it was impossible.

We made twenty miles today. Quite a change from what we did right after the storm. Perk thinks we should be in Springfield within ten more days. Kizzie says, first thing, she's going to have a grand and glorious washday. I'm going to find the post office and see if there's a letter from home. I shall feel awful if there isn't.

I hope Cousin Nathan and his family like me. I wonder what their house is like. It will be so nice to sleep under a roof again. I wonder how long I'll have to stay. My fondest hope is that I'll get a letter saying I only have to stay a few weeks for manner's sake and can come right back after that.

CHAPTER 29

Journey's End

November 9, 1837

"Is that Springfield?" Ruthy asked, when the scattered log buildings of a small town appeared on the horizon. She sat on a box just behind the wagon bench, looking out between Kizzie and Perk. A chilly wind blew clouds across the sky, tugged at Ruthy's bonnet brim and flapped the wagon cover.

"Don't know, for sure," Perk answered. "Can't you tell from looking at that fancy book of maps?"

"No, I can't," Ruthy said. "I looked last night. It doesn't have any towns this far out."

"Look," Kizzie said. "There's someone we can ask." She pointed a hundred yards or so beyond them to a man and woman on a slow-moving mule. The woman perched on a large stuffed bag tied behind the man's saddle.

As slow as their wagon train was, it moved faster than that old mule. When they drew alongside, the mule's rider pulled to a stop and the wagons did the same.

"Howdy," Perk said. "You folks from around here?"

"Naw," the man on the mule said. "We ain't. You'uns?

"No," Perk answered. "We're from Hawkins County, Tennessee, headed for Springfield, Missouri. We was wondering if that place up there was it."

The man on the mule looked off into the distance, then shook his head. "You couldn't prove it by me. We ain't got there yet. Who might you be?"

"I'm James Perkins," Perk answered. "This is my wife, Kizzie, and our friend, Ruthy Donohue."

The old man tipped his hat to the two women and said, "Mighty pleased, Ma'am, Miss. I be William Trower. Most folks call me 'Uncle William.'" He tilted his head back toward the woman behind him. "This be my missus, Phoebe. Phoebe says we're going to stop at the next settlement, no matter what it's called. I reckon she's right. We're plumb tired of traveling." He turned his head and spat a stream of brown tobacco juice on the ground. "Besides, this old mule, here, acts like he's on his last legs."

Phoebe nodded her head and smiled, but never opened her mouth.

The village they saw turned out to be Waynesville, county seat of Pulaski County. "Pulaski" sounded as strange to Ruthy as "Golconda" had, back in Illinois. But this time she had a chance to ask about it. She found out "Pulaski" was the last name of a Polish general who helped the colonists in the War for Independence.

They stopped in front of a large two-story log cabin. A bystander said it was the county courthouse.

"That thing's a courthouse?" Ruthy asked Kizzie, in a low voice. "It's nothing like as nice as the one we had, back home. Ours was brick and had a tower."

"I expect nothing is going to be much like it was before," Kizzie said. "But we'll make do. And who knows? We might just find our fortune out here."

"You and Perk may," Ruthy said. "But not me. I'm going to visit Cousin Nate for the littlest while I can and then go back where I belong. There might even be a letter saying I should turn right around and go home, when we get to Springfield."

Kizzie just nodded her head.

Soon, the wagons moved on down the rocky road.

"They said it's around eighty miles to Springfield," Perk told them as they jolted along. "Four or five more days and we'll be there."

Perk's estimate was right. They pulled into Springfield about mid-afternoon on the fifth day. Ruthy poked her head out between Kizzie and Perk, eager to see where they'd got to.

The first thing she saw was a large, square, open area with buildings all around the edge. Four stakes, marking the corners of a rectangle, stood upright in the ground in the center of the space. "Why do you suppose they put those posts in the ground?" Ruthy asked. Answering her own question, she said, "Maybe they're going to put a courthouse there. It looks like a good place for some kind of big building."

153

Without waiting for any kind of reply, she continued, "I wonder where the post office is." She stood and leaned farther out. "And, look, there's a creek over there. And they have more than one street. This place is actually beginning to look something like a town."

"Hush," Kizzie warned. "Folks ain't going to take it kindly if you look down your nose at where they live. It won't do you no good to start off on the wrong foot. My ma always said, 'If you can't think of something nice to say, don't say nothing a'tall.'"

"You two ladies can get down and look around a bit, if you want to," Perk said. "I have to ask where to park for the night and get some idea of the lay of the land. Keep a watch and if you see me standing here by the horses, come on back."

"I want to find the post office, first thing," Ruthy said. "And see if there's a letter from Mama and Papa."

The post office was another log cabin, located a block away, on a street called Jefferson, just past a cross street with a small sagging sign—Walnut.

Ruthy hurried in and asked if a letter had come for her. To her disappointment, the young man behind the half-wall dividing the public and private sides of the room didn't seem to be in as much of a hurry as she was. Instead, he stared at Ruthy. "Well, well. If it isn't another red head. You any kin to the Leepers?"

"Not that I know of," Ruthy said. "Who are they?"

"A family from Tennessee living out near Walnut Grove. A bunch of them have red hair just that color and I thought ..." His voice trailed off and he seemed to remember what he was supposed to be doing. He shrugged slightly and asked, in a more business-like tone, "I'll look for that letter right now. What name did you say, again?"

"Ruth Ann Donohue. It's been nearly two months since I left home. There should be one."

There wasn't.

Ruthy couldn't believe it. All this time she'd looked forward to a letter from home. That was the main thing that kept her going when she felt so lonely. She knew Mama would write. There must be some mistake.

"Could you look again?" she asked. "I know there ought to be one."

The postmaster looked again but didn't find anything. "Mail delivery is still chancy around here. It might be held up at Little Piney. We get it twice a month from a store up there. Or it might be on the way down from Booneville. I'll tell you what—why don't you check back in a couple of weeks? Maybe I'll have something then." He made as if to turn away.

"Ask him about your cousin," Kizzie reminded her.

"Oh, yes," Ruthy said. "Sir, do you happen to know a Mr. Nathan Graff? He's my cousin and he's supposed to meet me."

"I know him," the postmaster said. "But I haven't seen him in quite awhile. He lives out in the hills and doesn't come in very often. If you see him, tell him he has a letter. Been lying here for more than a month."

Ruthy's heart sank. She was afraid to ask the next question but felt she had to. "Could you check to see where it's from?"

After shuffling through a whole handful of mail crammed in a drawer, the postmaster said, "Here it is. It came from Tennessee." He held it up so Ruthy could look at it. The address was in her father's handwriting.

Ruthy turned away, shoulders sagging. Cousin Nathan didn't even know she was coming. What if something had happened to him? What if he'd moved on farther west? What was she going to do?

Kizzie put an arm around her young friend. "Don't look like that. Anything could have happened. We won't leave you until we find him. I promise." Kizzie began to move the two of them toward the door. "And your letter from your folks ... that's likely sitting right there in Little Piney, just like the postmaster said. You'll get it soon enough. Come on," she coaxed. "Things could be a lot worse. We're here and we're all alive and kicking. Let's go see what the merchants have for sale."

Ruthy let herself be steered back to the stores facing the public square. She missed her mama and papa so much. Everything here looked so new and rough and strange. And Cousin Nathan wasn't even expecting her. What if he and his wife didn't want company after all this time? There wasn't any way she could go back home this soon. If nothing else, she didn't have enough money to pay her way. She didn't know how much Papa had paid Perk, but she was sure it was a lot more than she had in her petticoat band. Face it, she was stuck, right where she was.

Nov. 12:

Nothing has happened the way I thought it would. It's so disappointing. All this way from home and no one to meet me. Perk and Kizzie can't wait here forever. They have lots else to do. If we can't find Cousin Nathan, I'll have to figure out something else. Either find a way to get back home or earn a living or something. I'm sure Mama and Papa didn't plan for me to be a servant but it may come to that. I'll probably have to sleep in a corner and work from daylight to dark for my daily bread. More than likely, I'll never see Mama and Papa again. It's too sad to consider. I won't say this out loud, but my stomach hurts at night from worrying.

CHAPTER 30

Cousin Nathan

The next days were busy ones. The small group of would-be settlers set up camp just outside of town. Perk found a man who knew where Cousin Nate lived—Mr. Cooper, his name was—and the man promised to stop by and tell the Graff family Ruthy had come.

Mr. Keeter took his leave to go on toward the west side of the county, in hopes of finding a good spot for his family to live. Ruthy could hardly bear to see him leave. He'd been a steady friend.

Before he left, he had a quiet word with Ruthy. "Miss Ruthy, if I find the right kind of place, I'll go back for my wife and children as soon as I can. Before I go, I'll check to see if you've found your cousin. If you need to send a message home, I can take that, too. Be sure to leave word at the post office as to your whereabouts."

Now she had two things to rely on. Kizzie and Perk had

158

promised to see that she was safe before they moved on and Mr. Keeter would check on her before he went back. Maybe it would be all right after all.

Mr. Grogan explored Springfield, trying to decide if there was room for another merchant. Will wanted to go, too, but had to stay by the wagons to protect the goods.

He moped about and complained until Ruthy said, "Will Grogan, I almost hope your father does decide to move on. At least I wouldn't have to listen to you complain anymore. If you want something to whine about, try coming all this way and not having anyone know you're coming. You don't hear me complaining, do you?" She kicked at the nearest wagon wheel and looked at the toe of her shoe, not daring to meet his eye. She would not cry. She wouldn't!

"You can complain if you want to," Will said. "I don't care. It's just so boring to have to stick around here all day with nothing to do. I wanted to go to town and see the sights, too. Why should Pa have all the fun?"

"He's not having fun; he's tending to business. And," Ruthy continued, "if you want something to do, why not take care of Feelie for awhile? Kizzie and I have plenty else to keep us busy. That old saying is right."

"What's that?" Will asked.

"Man works from sun to sun but woman's work is never done." At that moment, Kizzie called. "See what I mean?" she said.

Three days later, Mr. Grogan reluctantly decided to

move on. Springfield already had five merchants and that was more competition than he wanted.

"A Mr. Campbell, who's been here from the beginning, suggested I try Ash Grove or Walnut Grove," Will's father said. "He thinks I might be better off in a smaller community. That sounds right to me."

When the two wagons were hitched and ready to leave, Will said, "Well, Ruthy the Red, I didn't get to explore the town but I'm off to explore the wilderness. Watch out for wolves and bears. I hear they like red hair a lot."

His parting words were about what Ruthy could have expected. Still, her sudden pang of loss came as a surprise. "I—I—Don't wreck the wagon, Will," she stammered. "And next time you see me," she added fiercely, squaring her shoulders, "I'll thank you to call me 'Ruthy' without adding anything else." Turning her head, she flung out one last choked comment. "I'll miss you," she whispered, and hurried away.

The camp felt empty with only the Perkins wagon left. Ruthy's eyes strayed to the bare spots every morning and she wondered if Mr. Keeter and the Grogans had found what they were looking for. She even missed Will's teasing.

After a long week of waiting and worrying, Cousin Nate finally arrived, just about noon. Kizzie was dishing up when he came riding in on a large brown horse. Nate was nearly as tall as Perk and every bit as thin. He wore a brown homespun shirt and greasy leather pants held up by one suspender. A hole in the toe of his right boot was large enough for Ruthy to see that he wasn't wearing any socks.

"I'll bet a nickel one of you two ladies is Ruthy

Donohue," he said with a smile that made his blue eyes dance and his ragged appearance seem unimportant.

"Cousin Nate?" Ruthy said.

"That's me," he said, looking at her. "And ain't you the pretty thing! You've got your grandma's hair, right enough." He shoved his sweat-stained hat back to reveal his own hair, a slightly darker version of Ruthy's. "You can tell we're kin, can't you?

"I was out hunting when Cooper dropped by the house to say you was here. Didn't get back till yesterday evening. I came as soon as Hannah—that's my wife—told me."

Perk stood and extended his hand. "James Perkins."

"Nathan Graff," the newcomer said. "Ruthy's daddy's first cousin."

The two men shook hands and Perk said, "I believe we can stretch our dinner to cover one more. Will you eat?"

"Sure will," Cousin Nate said. He dropped to the ground in one easy movement, crossed his legs, and looked across the fire at Kizzie, with a warm smile for her as well. "If it won't put you out none, ma'am."

"Not a bit, Mr. Graff," Kizzie said, smiling in return. "But you'll have to take pot-luck, I'm afraid. It's nothing special." Kizzie portioned out the remaining beans, biscuits, and gravy as she spoke. Only Ruthy seemed to notice when her friend slipped an untasted piece of fried salt pork from her own plate to his.

Nate took his plate with a nod of thanks and began eating without another word. He speared the meat with the tip of his hunting knife and bit it off in huge chunks. He sopped his biscuit in the gravy and stuffed half of it in his mouth at

161

once, ignoring the large drop that fell on the front of his shirt.

"Mighty good grub, ma'am," he said when he finished, handing his empty plate to Kizzie. "Mighty good. Hunting as much as I do, being out in the woods and all, I don't get as much home cooking as I'd like." He re-crossed his legs and looked at Ruthy again.

"Now, tell me, Cousin. How's your daddy and them?"

Ruthy took a deep breath and had just opened her mouth to begin when Nathan sliced his hand through the air, cutting her off. "What am I thinking about? Don't tell me yet. We'll have time for talk on our way home. We'd better get moving. Got a lot of ground to cover before night falls. You ready to ride?"

Ruthy looked at Kizzie, uncertain in the face of his sudden hurry. "I guess so, but what about my chest? It has all my things in it. Did you leave your wagon somewhere?"

Cousin Nate stood. "Didn't bring one. Just come in on Chauncey." He motioned toward his horse. "Let's take a look at that chest." He strode toward the back of the wagon, Ruthy trotting along behind.

"Which one's your'n?" he asked, gazing at all the trunks and boxes.

"That one with the carving on the top, over there" Ruthy pointed. "I don't think Chauncey can carry it and me, too."

"No," Cousin Nate said. "He can't. Get what you need for now and we'll figure something else out later."

"Perk and Kizzie have to be going on," Ruthy said.

162

"Maybe we could leave it somewhere here in town and you could come in with the wagon in a few days and pick it up."

"Could," Nate said. "But can't. On account of, the front axle is broke and I ain't gotten around to fix it yet."

"Oh," Ruthy said. "Will it be hard to mend?"

"Naw, not if I put my mind to it. There's just so many other things I favor more, you see." He scratched his head, and frowned. "Maybe you better put a few things in a poke for now. A change of clothes and such like. Then, pretty soon, we'll come back in and get the rest."

Kizzie, standing just behind Ruthy, spoke up. "How long do you think that will be, Mr. Graff? Don't forget, winter's just around the corner. She'll need all her things by then."

"Not too long," Cousin Nathan said. "We'll work something out. I've been laying off to fix the wagon. Get that done, it won't be long a'tall." He laid his hand on Ruthy's shoulder. "Don't worry, Cousin," he went on, his voice suddenly gentle. "I know how much you ladies like your gewgaws and such-like."

Kizzie pursed her lips and sniffed. "Come on, Ruthy," she said. "Let's see what we can put together."

CHAPTER 31

Pioneer Homestead

At Kizzie's suggestion, Ruthy put on two layers of clothes: two pairs of drawers, two chemises, two petticoats, and two dresses. A lot of the drawstrings were stretched until there was hardly enough left to tie, and the last dress wouldn't button over everything else. She used her cloak to cover the gap.

"At least you'll have a change to wear on wash day," Kizzie said.

Ruthy tied up a few more things in a quilt—a nightgown, some stockings, a shawl, a comb, her journal, pen and ink, the unfinished sampler with needle and colored threads and her best petticoat with the coins in the band. Her hands lingered a moment over her books and the writing desk Papa made, but moved on. Books and wooden things were too heavy and bulky. Taking one last look at what she had to leave behind, Ruthy slammed the chest lid and straightened. "I guess I'm ready."

Wearing so many clothes made it awkward to get down from the wagon, but Ruthy managed, reaching up to take the quilt bundle before Kizzie also hopped to the ground.

The two young women stood quietly for a moment. Kizzie reached out and gripped Ruthy's shoulders. "Oh, honey," she said. "I can't hardly stand to lose you. I feel like I'm sending my little sister away. Are you sure you want to go? You could stay with us, you know. Maybe you ought to."

Ruthy ignored her own uneasiness. "Papa's known Cousin Nate since they were boys. He wouldn't have sent me if he hadn't felt right about it." She swallowed hard and tried to smile. "It'll work out. You'll see. He and his family are kin and I'm sure they'll take good care of me. Besides, it won't likely be all that long till I get to go back home."

Kizzie hugged Ruthy close. "I ain't never going to forget you. Never," she said. "Now, go, before I start bawling."

Cousin Nathan mounted Chauncey, reached down for Ruthy's hand, and pulled her up to sit behind him on the big brown horse. Kizzie handed Ruthy her quilt bundle and stepped back to stand by Perk, who was holding Feelie.

"All set?" Cousin Nathan asked.

"Yes," Ruthy answered, wrapping one arm around her cousin's waist.

"Then we're off," Nate said. He raised a hand to Perk and Kizzie. "Appreciate the dinner, ma'am. Don't worry none about this young'un. Me and the wife will be good to her. After all, she's kin."

A last wave, a click to Chauncey, and they began to move away, only to stop one more time at Kizzie's call.

"Wait," she said, running up to the horse. "What'll we do with the chest?"

"Oh, yeah," Nate said. "Best leave it at the post office, I guess." Another click to Chauncey and they were gone, away from the familiar wagon, across the creek, past the courthouse, out of the small town and on to wherever it was that Cousin Nate and Hannah lived.

After Ruthy began to get used to riding sideways, and the first awkwardness between two strangers had worn off, she asked, "Cousin Nate, do you want to hear about Papa and Mama now?"

He did and, as Ruthy told about her parents and her home, another wave of homesickness rolled over her and her voice choked.

"Hey, now," Nathan said, turning his head. "You ain't going to cry, are you?"

Ruthy squinched her eyes up tight two or three times, clutched her quilt bundle hard and sniffed. "I don't think so. It's just that I feel so far away and everything's so different out here."

"Not all that different," her cousin said. "Look around you. See that tree? It's a white oak. Same as back in Tennessee." He pointed from one side to the other. "Look at how we go up and down slope and across creeks. Didn't you do that back home? This is a good land. All the fish you can catch. All the meat you can shoot. Honey in the trees. Everything a body could want. You'll see. Pretty soon you'll feel better.

"And" he went on, "you're going to love my young'uns. Hannah and me got two living and another on the way."

166

"What are their names?" Ruthy asked.

"Nathan Harrison Graff, Jr.," Cousin Nate said proudly. "And Dorcas. Harry's six and Dorrie's two. That Harry has the makings of a real woodsman. He can already find his way back to anywhere he's been before. I took him squirrel hunting the other day and he did real well. Probably teach him to shoot this time next year."

"Did Hannah ... is that right? Hannah?"

"Yep."

"Did Hannah mind my coming?"

"Naw. Not a bit. Fact of the matter, she's glad to have another pair of hands. This time around, she hasn't done as well as usual. You'll be a big help, once the baby comes. And company, too. Now that you're here, I think I might see my way clear to being gone awhile." He shifted his seat in the saddle. "There's land west of here I ain't never seen and I sure would like to. Need to do some trapping, too. I can sell any pelts I get for cash money to pay taxes. I'm already late—supposed to pay up earlier in the fall, but with times the way they are ..." He sighed.

"You're going away?" Ruthy asked. He couldn't do that. Not when she just met him. Papa had counted on him to look out for her and keep her safe. He couldn't just up and leave. "What about my trunk?" she said.

"Oh, yeah. I keep forgetting your trunk," Nate said. "I need to get that before I leave. Tell you what, I'll start work on the wagon tomorrow morning, bright and early. And, Cousin, I'd take it as a favor if you wouldn't say anything to Hannah about me going trapping right yet. There ain't no use in worrying her ahead of time."

They rode on through most of the afternoon, pausing only once, when Ruthy said, "Cousin Nate, could we stop for a minute? I need to use the brush."

Nate stopped the horse immediately, saying, "I should've thought of that. Sorry. Here, hand me your bundle."

Ruthy slipped down and walked stiffly toward the nearest thick underbrush. She wasn't used to riding on the back of a horse.

"Watch out for snakes and poison ivy," Nate cautioned, carefully looking off toward the horizon.

Back on the trail, Ruthy said, "Tell me about your place."

That bit of encouragement seemed to be all her cousin needed. "It's a real nice piece of property," he said. "A wonderful spring and a creek. Lots of wildlife. Just enough rocks for chimbleys and things like that. I haven't gotten around to making a rock chimbley yet but I plan to. Plan to add on another room, too."

He paused and let his voice drop to a whisper. "Look yonder. Off to the left."

A deer with large antlers stood, completely still, between two trees. A moment later, with a flick of his white tail, he was gone.

"Ain't that one of the most beautifulest sights you ever seen?" Nate asked. "I never get tired of it. He really had a head of horns on him. Must have been ten, twelve points. Hang a lot of hats on them things."

"It was nice," Ruthy agreed. "We used to see them at home, too."

"Maybe not so often as here." Nate tapped his heels on Chauncey's side and they moved on. "Like I said, there's so much game in these parts, a man hardly has to work at all to keep his family fed. Not like back home, where my pa made us work in the fields from can till can't. I purely hated that. Of course," he reflected, "you've got your panthers and wolves along with the deer and the bear, but that's just a part of nature."

"You don't farm at all?"

"Oh, I farm, all right. Corn, mostly, for us and the hogs. But I don't spend my life doing it and I certain sure don't raise enough for a good cash crop. I depend on trapping and such like for cash."

The sun was touching the treetops when Ruthy smelled smoke.

"Nearly there," Nate said. Chauncey picked up speed without urging and they soon entered a small clearing. "Here we are," Nate said.

Ruthy peered around her cousin's broad back. Like so much else in this new place, it wasn't anything like Ruthy expected. In a clearing full of stumps stood a sad-looking little cabin with a mud and stick chimney leaning slightly off center. There were no front windows and no front porch. The only door opened directly onto a log step laid flat on the ground.

"It ain't much yet," Nate said. "Still, it's home. Let me hold your things while you get down." Ruthy slid from Chauncey's back, reached up and took her bundle from her cousin's hand, and stood waiting.

"Go right on in," Nate urged. "Hannah will be expecting you. I have to put the horse up and do the milking. Be there in a bit."

CHAPTER 32

Dirt Floor and Corn Shucks

Feeling abandoned, Ruthy watched Chauncey move out of sight around the end of the cabin, heading toward an unseen barn. The sun had fallen below the bare treetops and long shadows spread across the clearing. A chilly breeze swirled by and tried to lift her skirts.

"I'd better get moving," Ruthy told herself, "while there's still some light. If I don't, I'll probably stumble over every stump in this clearing." It felt awkward to walk up to a strange house and simply announce her presence. Cousin Nathan certainly was different from Papa; that was for sure. Papa would have gone in with her and put the horse up later.

Suddenly she felt something bump against the back of her knee and heard a whine. Looking down, Ruthy saw the strangest-looking dog she'd ever seen. He was black with white scattered here and there. One eye was blue and one was brown. His extra-long legs ended in paws so big they looked more like they belonged to a pony than a dog. One ear drooped so far down it nearly covered his blue eye.

Ruthy couldn't help but laugh. "Hello, ugly dog. What's your name? Are you friendly?"

At the sound of her voice, the dog yipped, stretched out both front legs and lowered his nose in a clear invitation. Ruthy laughed again. "You want to play. I don't have time right now, but I do have time to get acquainted." She made a fist and extended it. One smell of her fist and a single pat from Ruthy were enough to send the dog running in wide excited circles around the clearing, barking as he went.

The commotion finally brought someone to the cabin door. Two small heads peeked around the doorframe. It had to be Harry and Dorrie. Ruthy waved. Harry gave a small, shy wave in return. Dorrie ducked out of sight, then peeked back out again. It was enough to make Ruthy feel better. She picked up her quilt bundle and walked toward the house.

"What's your dog's name?" she asked, as she neared the door.

Neither child answered; they simply stood and stared.

Ruthy tried again. "My name's Ruthy. I'm your cousin and I've come for a visit. Your papa brought me out from town."

Still no response. These were certainly shy children. Should she go in? Should she wait for Cousin Nate? Or what?

171

A weak voice from inside solved the problem. "Come on in, Cousin Ruthy. They ain't used to strangers."

Ruthy stepped over the threshold, into the one-room cabin and onto a hard-packed dirt floor. The dog followed. A fire, flickering in the fireplace to her right, gave the only light. After her eyes adjusted to the dim interior, she could make out a table built of split logs, placed in the center of the room. Short logs standing on end served as stools. One was several inches taller than the others. In the far corner, on a bed attached to the wall, lay a thin-faced woman. Both children had scrambled back to stand beside her. The little girl sucked her thumb and held her mother's hand.

"Come closer, child. Let me look at you," the woman said with a tired smile. "You deserve a better welcome, but I've been feeling poorly lately."

Ruthy moved toward the bed. "Cousin Hannah?"

"Yes," the woman said. "And with that hair, you have to be Nate's cousin, Ruthy. Set your poke down and make yourself to home." Hannah struggled to a sitting position.

"Cousin Nate said you were in a family way," Ruthy said. "How soon?"

"About six weeks, I think," Hannah told her. "If all goes well. This one's been hard. But there, a woman's life is always hard." She stood slowly, and placed a hand in the small of her back, wincing as she did so.

"Can I help?" Ruthy asked, moving even closer.

Hannah waved her away. "No, I'll manage. Once I get started, I can generally keep going for an hour or so. Then, seems like I have to lay down again." She looked around the small room. "If I'd knowed sooner that you was coming, I'd have tried to fix things up a little. As it is . . ." Her voice trailed off.

"I'll do fine," Ruthy said. "After all those weeks in a wagon, I'm just glad to be here."

As she said that, Nathan came in from the barn carrying a bucket of milk, about half full. He set that down on the table. "I see you two ladies have struck up an acquaintance," he said. He stepped back outside, this time returning with two logs, one long and one short. Each was about three inches thick.

Dropping the logs just inside the door, he smiled at Hannah and sent her a questioning look of concern. Her nod was reassuring and he flapped a hand toward the corner opposite the bed. "What about putting her in that corner?"

To Ruthy, he added, "Hannah's been after me and after me to build another bed and I just never seemed to get around to it. These logs will do for now. I'll put them together after supper." He grinned and ruffled Harry's hair. "Think you can help me, boy?"

Supper included stewed squirrel in thick gravy, baked potatoes raked from the hot ashes, and pieces of wild plum leather. The sweet, chewy treat was new to Ruthy and she asked how it was made.

"Boil the plums till they're real mushy," Hannah said. "When they cool, reach in, feel around, and take out all the seeds. Boil it some more and sweeten it with honey." She reached out to stop Harry from grabbing the last piece of cornbread. "You've had enough," she said.

Looking back at Ruthy, she picked up her previous con-

173

versation. "When it gets thick, pour the mixture onto some flat boards and set them in the sun for three or four days. Keep a young'un out there when you can, to wave off the flies and wasps. Bring it in if it looks like rain. When it's dry as leather, roll it up and put it in a basket. It keeps good, if it don't get wet."

She wiped Dorrie's mouth with a corner of her apron and lifted the little girl down from her extra-tall log stool.

"Do you like it?" Hannah asked, looking at the leather with an anxious smile.

"Yes," Ruthy assured her. "I do. I'll have to remember to write the receipt in my housewife book. That is," she added, "when my trunk comes."

A thump from under the table reminded Ruthy. She looked at Harry again. "You never said—what's your dog's name?"

Harry ducked his head as before.

"Cat got your tongue, boy?" Cousin Nathan said. "Tell her."

"'Lysses," Harry murmured.

"YOU-lysses," Cousin Nate corrected. "On account of, that dog's a pure-dee wanderer. Always has been, from a pup. Somewhere back yonder when I wasn't much older than Harry, I remember hearing about a man from a long time ago who wandered all around. Name of Ulysses. So that's what we call the dog, when we can find him. Ain't as easy to say as 'Rover,' but he comes to it." Nathan chuckled. "Specially if he thinks there's something to eat when he does."

Ulysses' thumped his tail once more. Nate stood. "I'd better get going on that bed."

Curious about how two logs could become a bed, Ruthy watched Nathan every chance she got while helping Hannah put away the supper things.

It didn't take long. With Harry hovering at his elbow, Nate cut two notches in the log walls, just above the ground. The notch in the end wall was about three feet from the corner and the one in the front wall lay about five feet down from the same corner. Wedging an end of each log into a notch to hold it steady, he placed a wedge in the space where the two logs came together and fastened them with pegs. He'd formed a rectangular space, using walls on two sides and logs on the other two.

It looked to Ruthy as if she were going to sleep on the ground, even if she was inside a house. That wasn't much better than camping out.

Cousin Nate walked over to the bed on which Hannah had been lying earlier and gathered up a coverlet. "Back in a minute," he said.

Cousin Hannah stirred up the fire, put on two more logs, and sat back down at the table. Lifting Dorrie onto her lap, she said, "Now then, open up that pack of yours and let's see what you brought."

Ruthy did so. As each item came into view, Hannah touched it carefully with her work-worn hands and commented. "Your comb looks like new. Mine's as good as worthless. Ain't got enough teeth left to groom a fly."

"I like them colors," she said, as Ruthy unfolded her incomplete sampler. "What does that part, there, say?" She pointed to the verse.

"Right now," Ruthy said, "it only says 'Learning is a beauty bright / In learning I take great delight....' When it's finished, the rest will say, 'Beauty soon will fade away / But learning never will decay.' Then I'll put my name."

"That's nice," Hannah said

The last things Ruthy laid out were her journal with the pen and ink.

"Will you look at that?" Hannah stroked the journal's cover and turned a few pages. She looked around to locate Harry. He stood near the hearth, astride a thin stick with a string tied near the top, making clip-clopping sounds. "Harry, Cousin Hannah has a book. Come look."

Harry clicked to his imaginary horse, wheeled around, and trotted to the table.

"See?" Hannah said. "Your cousin wrote all this her own self. Someday, if we get a school around here, and you work hard, maybe you'll be able to write, too."

Harry stared at the journal with unblinking eyes, then returned to his play.

Hannah sighed. "Seems like, when you have a chance, you don't care for it. When you don't have a chance, like I didn't, you wish you could." She shook her head."

Nathan came back inside just then, bringing the coverlet, gathered into a pouch by its four corners and overflowing with dried corn shucks. He dumped the shucks into the space he'd outlined earlier and, kneeling, spread them out over the entire area. "There," he said, giving them a final pat. "One more load and a coverlet on top and you'll have a good bed. At least, it will serve until I get around to building a better one."

He stood and smiled. "Welcome to our house, Cousin Ruthy, such as it is. We're glad you're here." He dusted his hands together. "It's getting late and I've got to fix that wagon tomorrow. Let's put these two young'uns down and get to bed ourselves. Hannah, you need to show Ruthy where the privy is."

Hannah nodded and took Ruthy outside to the toilet. When they got back in, Nathan was already undressed and under the covers. The children were curled up together like two puppies, in a nest of quilts spread under the table. Ulysses had settled himself at their feet.

With the fire banked, Ruthy turned her back to the rest of the room, stood by her bed and began undressing in the dark. She took off her outer dress and unfastened the second one. At this point, feeling as if all eyes were watching in spite of the lack of light, she slid her nightgown over her head and finished taking off the rest of her clothes under its shelter.

Undressing like this was a new experience. Never before had she been forced to get out of her clothes with no privacy whatsoever other than what the darkness provided. Shivering, and wishing she had a second nightgown for warmth, she felt around for pegs on which to hang her dresses. There didn't seem to be any, so she folded the garments as best she could and stacked them on the ground. The dried cornshucks crackled when she lay down and rustled every time she moved.

The strange bed wasn't particularly uncomfortable but

177

Ruthy couldn't get to sleep. The harder she tried, the wider awake she became. Every small, unfamiliar night noise sounded loud to her ears. She heard Dorrie whimper in her sleep and Ulysses snuffle. She heard what sounded like a wolf howling.

Worst of all, Cousin Nathan snored—big, round sounds that began like the distant rumble of thunder, grew to a full-throated roar and ended with a snort, only to begin again with his next breath. Every snore seemed to rise to the rafters of the small room and bounce off the walls.

Ruthy wasn't sure how she'd ever get a decent night's sleep again if her cousin snored like this all the time. Her thoughts jumped from topic to topic with no hint of stopping even though she tried to shut them off. She was pretty sure this poor little cabin wasn't the sort of place Papa had envisioned when he sent her out here. For sure, he never thought Nathan would leave to go trapping right after she got here. If he actually did what he said.

What if the baby came while he was gone? Ruthy had heard that a father nearly always went and got a granny woman when a baby was about to come. And he wouldn't be here to go. She certainly wouldn't know what to do or who to call.

"If Papa knew what it was like here," she told herself, "he'd say I should come back home. I know he would. Mama would too."

CHAPTER 33

Cold, Harsh Light

Things didn't look any better next morning, in the cold, harsh light of the bright November day. If anything, seeing the inside of the cabin after sunup made Ruthy feel worse. Unfilled chinks between the logs allowed cold air to leak in. Cobwebs hung from the rafters next to drying onions. Sunlight crept between the curling shingles of the roof. What did they do when it rained?

So far as Ruthy could see, from her low-lying bed, Cousin Nathan and his family lacked most of the things she'd taken for granted in her own home. No pictures brightened the walls. The lone decorations, if you could call them that, were a few clothes hanging from pegs and her cousin's long rifle, resting on a set of deer horns above the door. Ruthy shuddered. At least he kept the gun up high, away from the children.

And big girls with quick tempers, she reminded herself.

179

Her eyes moved quickly over the rest of the furnishings. Except for the table with its stools, the only other pieces of furniture were a split-log bench, a single straight, hand-hewn chair with a woven bottom of dried leather strips, and a large wooden chest.

A lone flash of color on the mantel caught Ruthy's eyes at the very last. The china teapot with blue flowers painted on the lid sat in a place of honor above the fireplace.

Cousin Nathan's letter to Papa had sounded so cheerful. He mentioned recent hard luck, but there was no hint that they were this poor. Still, they seemed like nice people. That was something.

The sound of a chopping axe reminded Ruthy she'd better get up and dress while she had even a little bit of privacy because Cousin Nathan was sure to come in soon with an armload of wood.

Immediately after a quick breakfast of last night's left-over stew and hot cornbread, Cousin Nathan stood and said, "I'll be in the barn, Hannah, fixing that axle." He looked at Harry. "You want to go, son? I could use some help."

Harry nodded and followed his father out the door.

Ruthy spent the day getting acquainted with Hannah and Dorrie and learning how to fit into the family. She saw rather quickly why Cousin Nathan had been so glad to see her. Hannah wasn't feeling well at all and could hardly manage the most basic household chores. She must have made an extra-special effort to cook last night's supper.

"I'm sorry, Ruthy." Hannah said. "This ain't the way a body ought to treat company. I know better. I really do. I just can't do any better right now." Tears came to her eyes.

She glanced around to locate the children. Her voice dropped to a whisper. "I never felt like this with the others. Sometimes I wonder if I can bring this baby into the world alive." She placed her hand across her swollen belly. "I know for sure it doesn't move as much as the other two did."

Ruthy didn't know what to say. She didn't want to hear this. It was too scary. She'd heard whispers, when women got together back in Tennessee, of the hardships and dangers of childbirth. Girls always heard bits and pieces. But that was all—bits and pieces. Someone usually shushed the talker or sent the children outside. Still, even that little was enough to make her wonder, sometimes, why a woman would want to have a child in the first place.

Finally, she said, "Maybe everything will turn out all right."

When Cousin Hannah looked doubtful, Ruthy felt there was probably something else she should say but couldn't think what it was. So she changed the subject and asked, "What do you want to fix for dinner?"

Two days later, Cousin Nathan hitched up the wagon and drove to town. Before he left, he asked, "Do you want to send a letter home? Let them know you got here in one piece?"

Ruthy did. She tore a page from her journal and penned a quick note.

Dear Mama and Papa,

Cousin Nathan is about to leave for town, so I take this chance to let you know I have arrived safely and in good health. Cousin Nathan and Cousin Hannah have been very nice to me. I have not yet heard from you but hope to do so soon."

Your daughter,
Ruth Ann Donohue

Waiting for the ink to dry, she considered whether to add a bit more about what things were like but decided against it. They'd only worry and they certainly couldn't do anything about the situation from where they were.

Ruthy handed the letter to her cousin. "When you give this to the man at the post office, will you check to see if a letter has come from them?" she asked.

He said he would, and drove away, the empty wagon jouncing along over ruts and rocks.

Hours later, Nathan returned, bringing her chest, a length of rope, and another rifle. He set the chest at the end of her bed, laid the rifle and rope on the table, and reached into his pocket.

"I believe I may have something you've been wanting, Cousin Ruthy." He pulled a piece of folded paper from his pocket.

Her letter had come at last.

With great ceremony, Ruthy's cousin grinned, bowed from the waist and said, "Miss Donohue, it is my great honor to give you your letter."

Responding in the same spirit, Ruthy extended her hand and inclined her head. "Thank you, dear cousin," she said. Then, all pretense dropped, she clutched the precious paper to her chest, mumbled, "Excuse me," and ran outside.

Standing in the fading rays of the evening sun, she eased her finger under the green wax seal and broke it carefully. The second part of the letter was written crossways over the first part, to save space on the single sheet that could be folded, sealed, and mailed. It was a little harder to read that way but getting a longer letter was worth it.

Hawkins Co., Tennessee

Oct. 26, 1837

Dear Ruthy,

I am in receipt of three letters from you, each one gladly welcomed by your papa and me, as your presence is sadly missed. The last letter mentions bypassing a town called St. Genevieve, so I know you didn't get the one sent there. I trust this second one finds you well and in good spirits. Your journey sounds interesting. When next we are together, we shall have many things to discuss.

Papa finished his harvest but got very little return for the wheat. Hogs sold even lower than last year. I wonder if times are as hard there as here. At least our root cellar and smokehouse are full.

Sad to say, we still have not heard from Jesse.

I saw your friend, Josie, at church, Sunday last. Her mother now allows her to speak to me again. She says to tell you she longs for your company.

In answer to your request for a useful treatment for the

sick, I send the following: *For a cold in the head*, make a pot of hot chicken soup. Drape a warm cloth over the sufferer's head. Allow him to inhale the vapors. Then, serve a large portion, taken as hot as can be endured.

For cider cake: One pound and a half of flour, half a pound of sugar, quarter of a pound of butter, half a pint of cider, one teaspoonful of pearl ash to make the batter rise; spice to your taste. Bake in small loaves till it turns easily in the pans. I should think about half an hour.

Your papa sends his great affection, dear daughter, and tells you to be of good spirits. Feelings here seem to be settling down, so you may be able to come home sooner than we thought.

Remember to be helpful and kind and finish your sampler.

Your loving mother,
Martha Malloy Donohue

Ruthy read the letter three times, lingering over every word. For just a moment, she could almost hear her mother's voice. Then the cold wind, picking up at evening, made her shiver and reminded her she was far from home. Sighing, she folded the precious paper and went back inside the cramped building that was to be her new home—at least, for a little while. From the sound of things, it might not be too long.

"What did she say?" Hannah called from her bed, as soon as Ruthy stepped through the door. Three sets of eyes looked at her with interest. Even Harry sensed that the arrival of a letter was unusual, something to be shared.

Ruthy really wanted to keep her mother's words to herself a while longer but she gave in and read it aloud.

"So hogs aren't doing well there, either," Nathan commented when she finished. "I'm not surprised. I hear tell even the people up north are struggling."

"That cake receipt sounds good," Hannah said. "We have a couple of apple trees out back but they're still so little, they don't bear nothing."

"Did you see what I did while you was outside?" Cousin Nathan jerked his head in the direction of what the whole family had begun calling "Ruthy's corner."

Nathan had fastened the new rope across her corner of the room and hung a faded coverlet over it.

"I thought you'd like a bit of privacy, especially while I'm here," he said.

Ruthy looked at her cousin with a smile. "You think of everything, Cousin. Thank you."

He nodded and started to say something else but Hannah got ahead of him.

"While you're here?" she repeated, confusion in her voice. "What does that mean? You're not going to be here? Where are you going?"

Nathan explained his plan to travel west, trapping as he went. "That's why I took the loan of this here rifle from Cooper when I rode by his place. I didn't want to leave you without one. Those wolves we heard last night are likely to linger." He held up the extra muzzle-loader and added, "I told Coop I'd give him a day's work next spring for the favor. Clara said to tell you hello and that you should call her if you needed any help. I said you would."

By this time, Hannah was half-sitting, propped up in bed on one arm. "Nathan Graff, are you out of your mind? You can't go away on another one of your wild-goose chases. In case you ain't noticed lately, we've got a baby coming soon."

"Now, Hannah-girl," Nathan said. "That's six weeks from now. I'll be back in plenty of time. I'm not going all that far. If I'm lucky and the trapping is good, I'll bring home enough furs to pay last year's taxes and this year's too. I don't think the tax man will wait much longer."

He reached up to lay the borrowed rifle across the deer horns above the door, just below his own gun. "You don't want our land to be sold on the courthouse steps, do you? As far as I can see, this is the best chance I'll have, this trapping season. The crops—what there was of them—are in. Ruthy's here to be company for you. Everything will work out. You'll see."

Hannah sat completely upright, folded her arms, and shook her head. "Husband, sometimes I don't know what to make of you at all." She flopped down and turned her face to the wall.

Nathan stood for a moment, head bent. Then he moved to sit by her and began to stroke her back. It looked like such a private moment, Ruthy wondered if she ought to take the children and step outside, even if it was dark. Before she could move, though, her cousin began to speak. "I'll be back before you know it." His hand continued to stroke. "Just hold onto that. I may be a roamer, but have I ever failed to turn up when the chips were down? Have I? I promise you, it will be all right."

To Ruthy's relief, Hannah rolled onto her back again and looked at Nathan. "What if I asked you absolutely not to go?"

Nathan took her hand, turned it over, and traced the lines in her palm with his finger. "Hannah-girl, I have to. That man at the courthouse—the one we pay our taxes to—told me he couldn't carry us another year. What with two years of taxes at once and a third year coming up, I don't know any other way to get the money together. We can't afford to lose our land."

It wasn't her worry, exactly, but Ruthy couldn't keep quiet. "Cousin Nathan? I have some money. Papa gave it to me and I haven't spent any of it. Could you stay home if I gave you that?"

Nathan shook his head. "I can't take your money. Even if I did, it wouldn't be anywhere near enough. Not unless you're walking around with upwards of five dollars."

"That much?" Ruthy said. "Just to keep your own land? That's not fair."

"Maybe not," Nathan answered. "But that's the way it is. The tax collector always has the last word." He patted Hannah's hand one last time and stood. "No use putting it off. Sooner I start, the sooner I'll get back. I'll get my things together and try to get off day after tomorrow."

CHAPTER 34

Danger at the Door

"Ruthy, do you know how to milk a cow?" Hannah's voice woke Ruthy up, early the morning after Nate left.

Ruthy poked her head out from under the quilts. "Just barely," she called. "Why?"

"Well, we have to take care of it, now that Nathan's gone, and I'm not sure I can, today," Hannah said. "I don't feel well at all."

Ruthy sat up, scratched her head, blinked and yawned. "Let me get dressed," she said, and yawned again. She hurried into her clothes and walked to her cousin's bedside.

Hannah's face was drawn and without its normal color.

"What's wrong? Is the baby coming?" Ruthy's voice sounded anxious, even to her own ears.

"No," Hannah said. "Not yet, thank goodness. I just don't seem to have any strength." Tears filled her eyes. "If

188

only Nathan hadn't picked right now to go off on one of his excursions."

"I'm surprised he did," Ruthy said. "He ought not to have left you at a time like this." She almost added that her papa wouldn't have acted like that, but caught herself.

"He's not a bad man," Hannah said. "He loves us and does the best he can. He just doesn't always stop and think."

"Well, he ought to," Ruthy said, ignoring her own, similar, fault. She wrapped her arms about herself and shivered. The cabin was cold. When Nathan was here, he always got up first and built the fire. It really made a difference.

"Let me get the fire going," Ruthy said. "Then I'll do what I can about the milking." She looked toward the children still in bed under the table. "Harry, can you help me out at the barn?"

Without a word, the small boy crawled out from under the table. He'd slept in his clothes.

"Where's your shoes?" Ruthy asked, eyeing his dirt-encrusted feet. "It's cold outside."

"Ain't got none." Harry whispered.

"We was going to get him some when we sold the crops," Hannah hurried to explain. "But it was a bad year. Son," she added, raising her voice slightly, "Your papa is counting on you to be a big boy. Get yourself and Dorrie up and help your cousin."

Ruthy thought again of the coins in her petticoat. How much did shoes for a little boy cost? It was tempting to stand and think of all she could do if she were rich, but that didn't get the fire built. Or the cow milked either.

Sighing, she moved across the room, knelt down and raked the ashes away from the live coals in the fireplace. She placed some kindling on top and blew on the coals until they glowed. When the smaller pieces of wood began to smoke, she sat back on her heels and watched the fire begin to blaze. The warmth felt good.

Putting on enough wood to last awhile, Ruthy picked up the milk bucket, held out her hand for Harry and walked outside. She looked around for the cow, but couldn't see her.

"Harry, where's the cow?" she asked.

Harry pointed to a small pasture enclosed with a rail fence. Ruthy looked but couldn't see the animal.

"Where?" she asked again.

When Harry pointed the second time, Ruthy set the bucket on the ground. Crouching before the boy, she took hold of both his shoulders and looked into his eyes. "Harry, you have to talk to me. I know you can. You told me about Ulysses. Remember?" She gave him a small shake. "Don't just point. Use words. Where is the cow?"

Harry stared back at Ruthy and smiled. "In the pasture," he told her. "hiding behind the barn."

Ruthy stood, picked up the bucket again, and smiled in return. "That's better. Thank you. Do you know how to bring her in?"

"Yes."

"Please do it then, while I put some hay in the manger."

Soon, the cow was in her stall, tied up with a thin rope, and chewing a mouthful of hay. Ruthy eyed the animal with doubt. Some cows kicked. She hoped this cow wasn't one of those. Well, she'd soon see. Placing the bucket carefully, she

190

squatted to begin, only to be stopped by a poke in her shoulder. It was Harry.

"Ain't you going to send me for water to wash her off?" he asked.

She'd forgotten. Papa always washed off the cow's udder before he milked. It kept the milk cleaner. While she waited for Harry to return from the spring, she stroked the animal's neck and talked to her in a soft voice. It might make the cow more comfortable.

Harry staggered in with a full bucket of water, almost too heavy for his thin arms. Ruthy hurried to take it, and sloshed water on the cow's udder from both sides until the bucket was empty. Now it was time to milk.

She could do this, she thought. She'd watched her brothers and her father milk many times, and she'd tried it, herself, once or twice.

Squatting down again, she placed the empty bucket beneath the cow, wrapped her hands around the two nearest teats, and pulled. Nothing happened. Not a single drop of milk came out. She tried again. Still nothing.

Harry giggled softly. Ruthy glared at him. "Can you milk?" Harry shook his head.

"Then hush," she said and tried again, squeezing harder. This time she was rewarded with a tiny white stream. "Good girl," she called to the cow, reaching up to give the animal's hip a pat. Leaning her head into the cow's side, she grabbed hold and pulled again. More milk. It didn't take long to find a rhythm and soon the bucket was half-full of frothy milk.

"We'll leave the rest for the calf," Ruthy said as she stood.

Harry led the cow back to the pasture, where her small calf waited, hungry for his share. Ruthy took the milk into the house.

"You sure was gone a long time," Hannah said, now up and sitting by the fire with Dorrie in her lap. "Did Maizie give you trouble?"

"So that's her name," Ruthy said. "Maizie. I'll use it next time." She set the bucket on the table and rubbed her forearms. Milking took muscles she didn't normally notice. "No. I'm just not used to milking and I'm slow. I'll get faster."

Hannah kissed Dorrie, set her down, and handed her a doll made of cornhusks. "Play with Dolly," she said, and patted her head, then looked up at Ruthy and smiled weakly.

"I hate I had to ask you. I don't know what I'd do, right now, though, if you wasn't here."

She nodded toward the corn pone, soft butter, and honey sitting at the other end of the table. "You ain't et, yet. The honey's good. Nathan robbed a big bee tree last winter and we still have quite a bit." She stood with effort and dragged the chair nearer to the table. "I think I can make shift to strain the milk, sitting right here, if you'll fetch me that pan hanging over there and the cloth next to it."

Ruthy did as Hannah asked. She'd just taken her first bite of buttered pone with honey when Harry, Ulysses on his heels, burst into the house and slammed the door. The small boy's face was pale, his eyes sparkled with excitement, and his chest heaved.

"Mama! Ruthy! There's a wolf out yonder, walking crooked." He re-opened the door a crack and peered back outside. "He's just standing there, Mama. Right out in the middle of the clearing, in broad daylight. And he looks mean. He growled at 'lysses and me. We ran."

Hannah set the milk bucket down, stood, and walked slowly to the door, holding her back. As soon as she looked out, her eyes squinted and her hand flew to her mouth. "Oh, my law."

Ruthy swallowed her food with a gulp and jumped up. "A wolf? Right out there? Let me see."

She hurried to take a look. "Poor thing, he's trembling." She looked at Hannah. "I think he's sick, Hannah. Do you suppose he came to us for help?"

"No!" Hannah replied sharply. She closed the door firmly and dropped the bar. "He's going mad. I'm sure of it. He's not acting normal at all. Did you notice if he was foaming at the mouth or not? I can't see good, that far away."

Ruthy hurried over to peek through one of the spaces between the logs where the chinking had fallen out. "It's hard to tell. But his mouth's wide open. I see his tongue." She put her eye back to the open space. "He's coming closer." She moved back and motioned. "Look, Harry. He can't even walk straight."

"Harry. Ruthy," Hannah said. "Both of you. Look at me." She waited until both sets of eyes met hers. "Don't either one of you dare go outside, you hear me? When animals are like that, they ain't theirselves. That wolf would just as soon come at you as not. And if he bites you, you'll take hydrophoby, just like he has, and you'll die! Did Ulysses get anywhere near him?" she asked, looking at her son.

Harry shook his head, put his arm around the dog standing nearby, and pulled him close.

Ruthy and Hannah stared at each other with dread.

"What are we going to do?" Ruthy whispered. "Do you think he'll go away?

"I don't know," Hannah said. "I never saw a rabid animal in the wild. I did see a mad dog, once, a long time ago. He acted just like this. Somebody shot him."

Ruthy's eyes lifted to the muzzle-loader above the door and quickly looked away.

Suddenly, Hannah walked to the chair and sat down abruptly. She placed her hand over the large mound beneath her apron and winced. "I do believe," she said, "that this baby is on its way."

CHAPTER 35

Someway, Somehow

"It can't be coming yet," Ruthy said. "It hasn't been six weeks. You said six weeks."

"That's what I thought, but babies come in their own time."

Ruthy twisted her hands together and looked wildly around the room. "Hadn't you better lie down? Do you need any help?"

Hannah shook her head. "Not yet. It takes awhile." She straightened her shoulders. Her body seemed filled with purpose. "We need to go tell Mrs. Cooper. She said she'd come when it was time. Harry can do that. He knows the way. " Hannah's eyes roamed from the bed to the water bucket to the fire. "You'd better fill the water bucket and the kettle, Ruthy."

"I can't" Ruthy said. "The wolf. Did you forget?"

Hannah rubbed her forehead. "I did, for a minute." She gnawed on her lower lip.

"I could throw rocks at him, Mama," Harry said. "Me and 'Lysses could make him go away."

"No, you couldn't," Hannah told him sharply. "You remember what I said, young man! That wolf has hydrophoby. If he bites you, you'll die. You stay in this house. I've got enough to think about without that."

Again, Ruthy's gaze wandered to the rifle above the door. Hannah's eyes followed hers.

"Hannah, can you shoot the gun?" Ruthy asked. "That's why Cousin Nathan left it here. In case something like this happened."

"He only did that to make hisself feel better about leaving," Hannah said. "He knows, better than most, how short-sighted I am. I couldn't hit the broad side of a barn in bright daylight."

"Maybe you wouldn't have to," Ruthy said. "Even if you missed him, the noise might scare him off." She couldn't bring herself to mention her own shooting lessons, back home. If she never picked up a gun again as long as she lived, it would be fine with her.

Hannah shook her head. "I doubt it." Her face creased as another pain came. She stood. "Harry, I need you to be mama's big boy. Come here, son, and lend me your shoulder."

Harry came, eyeing his mother anxiously. Hannah rested one hand on her son's shoulder and the two began to walk slowly, up and down the length of the cabin.

Ignored, Dorrie chose that moment to set up a howl. Ruthy picked her up, hugged her close, and began to sway back and forth. Dorrie saw her mother over Ruthy's shoulder and stretched out her hands. "Mama, Mama," she cried.

"Sh-h-h. Don't cry, sweet girl. You're all right." Ruthy swayed faster and whirled around. "Whee-ee! We're going round and round!"

Dorrie kept crying.

Ruthy looked toward Hannah. Maybe she knew what Dorrie wanted. But Hannah didn't notice. She was completely focused on her walking.

How is it, Ruthy wondered, that I always end up with a crying child when things go wrong? First Feelie, now Dorrie.

The howls changed to pitiful sobs. The little girl kept reaching out toward her mother.

As if to keep company with Dorrie's wailing, Ruthy's stomach growled loudly, reminding her she'd had only one bite of breakfast. Still jiggling Dorrie, Ruthy moved toward the other end of the table and picked up the piece of cornbread she'd smeared, earlier, with butter and honey. She took a bite. It was cold and dry, but anything would have tasted good, right then.

Dorrie stopped reaching for her mother and pointed to what she saw Ruthy eating. "Me, me," she sobbed.

"Is that what you want?" Ruthy asked. "Bread and butter and honey? Why didn't you say so? Here." She broke off a small piece and held it to Dorrie's mouth. Dorrie ate it and opened her mouth for more. Several bites later, she finally allowed Ruthy to set her down. The minute Dorrie's feet touched the floor, she ran to her mother, took Hannah's outstretched hand and did her best to keep up as the three of them kept walking.

Freed of the child, Ruthy opened the door a crack and

peeked out to see what the wolf was doing. He was staggering around the clearing, growling fiercely at unseen threats, stopping now and then to turn in circles and bite at himself. His mouth drooled freely.

"Die, wolf," she muttered. "Die. Or go away. One or the other."

"What time is it, Ruthy?" Hannah asked.

Ruthy looked at the sun. "Nearly noon, I think. The sun's overhead." Her eyes followed Hannah as her cousin kept walking—up and down, up and down.

"Are you sure you ought to keep walking, Hannah? Don't you think you ought to lie down and rest?"

"I'm walking," Hannah said, "because that's what the granny woman who came when I had Dorrie said to do. She said it made things easier. And I have to admit, Dorrie came easier than Harry." She stopped, pressed her hand to the bulge beneath her apron, and breathed hard.

"Ruthy, we can't wait much longer to send for Mrs. Cooper. At first, I could sing *Old Hundred* in my head five times between pains. Now I'm down to three." She looked at Ruthy, worry in every line of her face. "I don't know what to do. Have you ever seen a baby born? Looks like you're going to have to help me."

Horrified, Ruthy stared at Hannah. She couldn't do that. She absolutely could not do that. She wouldn't have the slightest idea how to help. She'd never even seen Molly have puppies. Papa said it wasn't fitting. How could she help with a baby? They would have to get Mrs. Cooper.

She walked to the door and peeked out at the wolf again. "He's still there," Ruthy said. "You should see him. He

198

keeps dashing one way, then the other. Now he's turning in circles and biting himself. And he's slobbering something awful!" She drew back.

Ulysses crowded in next to her knee, stuck his nose to the crack and gave a fierce growl. The wolf looked up, snarled in return and made a dash toward the cabin. Ruthy slammed the door and dropped the bar as quick as she could. Ulysses jerked away, barely in time to avoid a bruised snout.

Heart thudding in her chest, Ruthy closed her eyes and stood for a moment with her head resting on the closed door. The rifle above her weighed on Ruthy's mind as heavy as a wagonload of rocks. The gun was a flintlock, just like Papa's. A leather pouch with the necessary powder, patches and bullets hung nearby.

All she'd have to do would be load it, stick it out the door, cock, aim and shoot.

Her mind knew what she ought to do, but every time she considered it, something deep inside her could only see a dead boy lying in the front yard, back in Tennessee. The horror of the memory made her reluctant even to lift the rifle down from its perch, much less deliberately aim to kill. A target like a tree was one thing; a living being—even a sick wolf—was another.

She hunched her shoulders, laid a sweaty palm on Ulysses' head and turned back to the room. The bucket of milk still sat on the floor where Hannah had left it, a million years ago. Feet dragging, Ruthy moved to pick it up.

Somehow, someway, she had to get through the rest of this awful day. But she didn't see how.

CHAPTER 36

Hit or Miss

"Ruthy," Hannah said. "There's things I've got to tell you before the pains get any worse—things you'll need to do."

"What?"

"First thing, look in the chest. There's a piece of flannel, some diapering cloth, and some other stuff laying in the tray on top, at the right hand end. I laid them there special. Get it all out and put it on this end of the table, where you can reach it after the baby comes."

Ruthy walked to the large wooden chest she'd noticed earlier and lifted the heavy lid. She scanned the contents of the tray in the top of the chest. A small wooden box, a sewing kit, a bit of dark blue yarn and three knitting needles, what looked like some odds and ends ... there they were, the things Hannah wanted.

200

"What next?" Ruthy asked, laying the items on the table.

"Let me see," Hannah said, holding onto the table with one hand and sorting the stack with the other. "Flannel to wrap the babe, diapering cloth, an extra sheet to put under me, string—that's to tie the cord, don't lose that—and we'll need the kitchen knife to cut the cord after it's tied." She pointed to a small shelf on the left side of the fireplace. "See it? Better wipe it off with the dishtowel. We would be low on water just when it's needed. I wish my scissors hadn't broke."

Feet dragging, Ruthy retrieved the knife and looked at the sharp blade. "Cut the baby? That doesn't sound right."

"You don't cut the baby, only the cord, after you've tied it off. You have to tie it in two spots and cut between. I might be able to do that. We'll see."

"The calf had a cord," Harry piped up. "When it was born. It hung down from his belly. I saw it."

Hannah looked at Ruthy and rolled her eyes. "This child never remembers the rule about children being seen, not heard."

She grabbed the table with both hands again, as the next pain hit. After it was over, she said, "I've lost count, but I think I'd better lie down."

Leaning on Harry, she walked to the bed, showed Ruthy how to arrange the extra sheet, and stretched out.

Ruthy checked on the rabid wolf again. Nothing had changed, except the shadows were longer and the wolf seemed a little closer to the house. It was a shame this cabin didn't have a back door, she thought. Then Harry could slip out without the wolf even knowing.

"Be praise and glory evermore." Hannah finished her chanting method of telling time. "Still there?" she asked.

Ruthy nodded.

Hannah clenched her eyes tight shut for a moment, breathed hard through her mouth, then continued. "Get Dorrie and put her up here by me, will you?" She reached out a hand for Harry and, when both children were settled, she said, "Your mama is going to make a lot of noise after awhile. It's going to sound real scary. I wish you didn't have to hear it, but there isn't any place safe for you to go." Her attempted smile was weak. "Try not to let it scare you. Keep remembering, after all the noise, you'll have a new baby brother or sister.

"And never forget, your mama loves you very much." She looked directly at her son. "Harry, you'll be sure to re-member what I said and tell Dorrie, if needs be? You won't never let her forget?"

"I won't, Mama." Tears rolled down his cheeks.

She wiped Harry's cheek with her hand and hugged Dorrie. "Ruthy, hang the coverlet back across your corner. Put these two behind it. I hate to have them in here but I don't know what else to do. Harry, don't let Dorrie come out, no matter what. Hold her tight if you have to and don't let go, even if she screams."

That done, the next directions were for Ruthy's ears only. "When the baby comes out, it's going to be pretty messy. Don't pay that no mind. We can clean up later. First thing, tie the cord tight with the string, then tie it again, a little farther on. Cut the cord between the ties.

Ruthy gulped. "I can't do this," she said again, shaking her head. "I keep telling you, I can't do this."

"You have to," Hannah said. "There ain't nobody else.

"Now listen to me! This is important. Once the cord is cut, pick the baby up by his feet. Hang him upside down, and swat his bottom. We want him to cry so he'll take his first breath. He has to start breathing. He's early and he'll be real little. Don't pay that no mind, neither. Just give him a good swat. If that don't work, do it again."

Ruthy hugged her arms tightly across her chest and continued shaking her head, trying her best not to burst into tears. First she had to cut something, then she had to hit the baby. It was too much. Cousin Hannah had no right to ask it of her. There had to be another way.

Actually, there was, if she had the nerve. Her eyes strayed, as before, to the deer horns above the door. She took a deep breath. Voice shaking, she said, "Cousin Hannah, there's something I didn't say awhile ago."

"Can it wait?" Hannah asked through gritted teeth. Her knees were drawn up and she had her feet flat on the cornshuck mattress.

"I don't think so. I think I have to tell you. You see, I know how to shoot a rifle. Papa made me learn. But I don't want to do it. I'm afraid of killing something."

Or somebody, she added silently.

"Well, it's that or catch the baby. You decide. I can't think about it." Hannah resumed chanting, pausing now and then to grab her belly and moan. "Him serve with fear, his praise foretell ..."

"Ruthy," Harry called from behind the coverlet.

Ruthy lifted a corner of the quilt. Harry was in tears again. "Sister wet her britches. She couldn't help it. She needed to go real bad. I do, too." He looked up at his cousin. "Is Mama going to die?"

"Not if I can help it." Ruthy hurried to the bed, stooped, and pulled a white clay pot from underneath. "Here," she said, thrusting it at Harry. "Use this. I didn't think. It's all right about Dorrie. Just keep her there. Remember what your mama said. Don't let her get away."

Somewhere between Hannah's bed and the pitiful look on Harry's face, Ruthy made up her mind.

Without pausing to consider further, she strode to the door, grabbing the chair as she went. She climbed onto the chair seat, lifted the rifle from its perch, and stepped back down. Next, she checked the flash pan to be sure it was empty, and reached for the bullet pouch.

"*Pour a measure of powder down the barrel.*" Papa's directions echoed in her ears.

"*Wrap the bullet in a patch and ram it down the barrel, too.*" She did that and replaced the ramrod.

"*Cock the gun halfway, pour some powder in the flash pan, and stop to look beyond.*"

Holding the gun carefully, Ruthy opened the door. The wolf stood in the middle of the clearing, head down, legs spraddled. Ruthy lifted the gun to aim it. She'd forgotten how heavy it was. It wouldn't stay steady. She'd have to prop it on something.

She closed the door and moved to a gap in the chinking. Would there be a view of the wolf through this hole? Yes. She shoved the barrel out the hole and squinted over the sights.

"*Wait. Look beyond.*"

Nothing there but trees, with their lengthening shadows. And the sun, getting lower in the sky with every half-hour that passed.

"*Put the gun on full cock. Take a deep breath, let it out halfway. Squeeze the trigger.*"

BAM! The powder flashed, the gun fired, and recoiled with a hard, bruising jolt. Ruthy had forgotten to snug the butt tight enough into her shoulder. Ears ringing from the blast, shoulder aching, she blinked and peered out, ignoring Harry's shout, Dorrie's wail, and Ulysses' frantic barking.

The wolf was unhurt. Still swaying and slobbering, he'd simply moved a small distance away and stopped. The bullet had missed him entirely.

Harry came out of his corner, dragging Dorrie by one hand. "Did you shoot the wolf? Is he dead? Let me see."

"There's nothing to see. I missed him entirely. Get back," Ruthy said. "And get Dorrie back too."

Making a face of disgust, Harry dragged his sister back halfway to where he was supposed to be.

Ruthy waited until the two children had moved away and began to reload. "I'll get him on this try," she muttered. This time, she held the gun more tightly to her shoulder. She aimed as carefully as she knew how and fired again. BAM!

She missed again. All she had accomplished was to move

the wolf still farther away. But not far enough to allow Harry to go for Mrs. Cooper.

Ruthy leaned her head against the wall.

"Did you shoot better this time?" Harry asked. He started to move up again but Ruthy's upraised hand stopped him.

"No," Ruthy said. "But third time's a charm. I'll try once more."

She never got that third chance.

A muffled cry from the far corner recalled Ruthy's attention to the situation inside the house. She leaned the rifle against the table and moved toward Hannah. Halfway across the room, she remembered what she'd just done. Shaking her head at her own carelessness, she retraced her steps and returned the rifle to its place above the door.

"Ruthy." A second strangled call sent Ruthy scurrying to the bedside, wondering what hard thing she'd have to do next. Whatever it was, she knew it wasn't going to be good.

CHAPTER 37

Life and Death

"The young'uns," Hannah said through clenched teeth when Ruthy reached her side. "Don't let them see this. It'll scare them to death. They won't understand."

Wishing she could hide in a corner as well, Ruthy turned her head to check on the two children. Harry's eyes peered around the coverlet-curtain. "Your mama said to get back, Harry," she told him. "Now do it."

"Don't want to," Harry whispered, tears welling up again.

Ruthy knew exactly how he felt. "I know," she said. "But do it anyway. Dorrie will be even more scared if you don't stay with her."

She turned back to Hannah. "Tell me what to do. I don't know how to help and I'm scairt. Is the baby about to come?"

Hannah couldn't talk. Ruthy watched while her cousin dug her heels into the mattress, yelling and straining until her face was red. When that stopped, she panted from the

207

effort. At last she said, "It's coming, I think. Look. Can you see the top of its head?"

Ruthy looked. "No."

"Are you sure?" Hannah asked.

"I'm sure."

After several more hard pushes, Ruthy looked again. "I see something. It looks like the top of a head. Push some more."

As Ruthy watched and Hannah kept pushing, the whole head gradually appeared. The baby was coming.

"What do I do now?" Ruthy yelled.

"Put your hands under it," Hannah said. A bit more hard work, along with a couple of loud screams and one last mighty push, the baby slipped out. It was wet, bloody, and covered with some whitish stuff. Its eyes were tightly shut, and it was a girl.

"It's a girl!" Ruthy said.

"Another girl," she heard Harry say, his voice filled with disgust.

Hannah lay still, her eyes closed. Sweat plastered her hair to her forehead.

No wonder they call it labor, Ruthy thought. From what she could tell, having a baby took more effort than working all day in the field. Plus, it looked like it hurt. A lot!

Still not opening her eyes, Hannah whispered, "Alive?"

"I don't know," Ruthy said. She looked at the newborn, lying there. It wasn't breathing.

"Tie the cord." Hannah's voice was hardly louder than a breath.

Ruthy got the string and tied the cord in two places. She

couldn't quite bring herself to use the knife, though. It seemed so awful. Hannah had said she might be able to do it but one look at the exhausted woman told Ruthy it was up to her.

She took a deep breath. Her hand trembled. "You have to do it," she muttered. "You have to." But it was so hard. Harder than firing a gun. Harder than leaving home. Harder than anything she could imagine. "You have to," she repeated, a little louder.

Feeling bile in the back of her throat, Ruthy clenched her jaw, set the knife and made the cut where Hannah had said, between the two knotted ties. "Oh, Baby," she said. "I'm so sorry."

The baby lay still. She looked a little gray. Was she dead? What if she was dead? Close to panic, she suddenly remembered Hannah had said to pick the infant up and spank its bottom.

After cutting the cord, a spanking didn't seem hard at all. Ruthy picked the baby up by its heels. Its skin was so slippery, she thought for a minute she might drop it on its head, but she didn't. She held on and gave the little bottom a sharp swat. A series of weak cries rewarded her efforts. The baby was breathing.

"Did you hear, Hannah?" she called. "She's alive."

A single gunshot outside the cabin, followed a few minutes later by a thunderous banging on the door, punctuated Ruthy's delight in the baby's cries. Clutching the infant close, she called, "Who is it?"

"It's Cooper, miss. Can I come in?

Harry didn't wait for permission. He scurried to the

door and lifted the bar. "Hi, Mr. Cooper. I heard a shot. Was that you? Did you kill the wolf?"

Mr. Cooper stepped inside, smiled and ruffled Harry's hair. "Yep. He's deader than a buzzard's dinner." He looked toward Ruthy and beyond. Then, quickly, his ears turning red, he turned to the fireplace.

Ruthy saw his embarrassment. Still clutching the baby, she hurried to tear the coverlet curtain off the rope with one hand and toss it over Hannah's lower body. "I tried to shoot him, myself," she said, hurrying back to the center of the room. "So Harry could go get help." She grabbed the bit of flannel off the table, wrapped it around the small body in her arms and continued. "But I missed him both times."

"I heard two rifle shots," Mr. Cooper explained, "and figured something was wrong." He took off his hat. "We ain't met, but I'm Cal Cooper, the neighbor. I was the one what came and told Nate you was here."

Ruthy nodded her head. "I know, and I truly appreciate it."

Mr. Cooper put his hat back on his head. "When I got here and seen what the problem was, I took care of it right away. You're lucky nobody got bit. I've saw mad dogs and mad skunks, but I ain't never seen a mad wolf before."

He looked at the baby and smiled. "Looks like you've had your fill of trouble. Boy or girl?"

"Girl," Ruthy said. "Hannah was so brave. She did it all by herself." She looked down at the baby. "Well, nearly all of it. I cut the cord."

Now the emergency had passed, Ruthy's face crumpled. She sank onto the nearest log stool. "I was so scared, Mr.

Cooper. And I don't know what to do now. She's so little, she barely cries. And Hannah doesn't look good. Please, can Mrs. Cooper come?"

Mr. Cooper tugged his hat a little tighter and started for the door. "Harry, don't you touch that wolf, son. He's still dangerous. I'll take care of him later. Right now, I have to ride. Be back as fast as my horse can move. Hang on."

CHAPTER 38

Unexpected

As soon as Mr. Cooper left, Ruthy hurried to Hannah's bedside.

Harry ran ahead. "Did you hear, Mama?" Harry said. "Mrs. Cooper's coming, and Mr. Cooper kilt that wolf. Shot him dead as dead! "

Hannah licked her lips. "Good," she said. Her voice sounded hoarse. She raised her arms. "Ruthy, would you give me the baby? I ain't held her yet."

Ruthy put the infant in Hannah's outstretched hands, unprepared for the emptiness she felt in her own arms as soon as she handed the baby over. Both Ruthy and Harry watched Hannah examine her scrawny, wrinkled daughter. The little mite opened her mouth, made a few sucking motions, and began to wail.

"She sure is ugly, Mama," Harry said. "Maizie's calf

looked a lot better than that when she was born. How come she don't have no hair?"

Hannah smiled. "She's barely alive yet. Give her time. You didn't look real pretty yourself, when you was borned."

She pulled the baby's flannel wrap tighter and cuddled her close, then smoothed the top of the hairless head. "Slick as goose grease," she said. "That's all right, Baby. It will grow."

"She's so little," Ruthy said. "What's her name? I hate to keep calling her 'Baby.'"

"We haven't picked one out yet. I favor Jennie, but Nate's partial to Abigail. That's his mother's name. There's no rush. I always like to wait and see if they're going to live. Hate to waste a name on a burial stone. I guess we'll decide when Nathan gets back."

Hannah's eyes strayed to Ruthy's bed in the far corner. "Dorrie," she called. "Honey, come see your new sister."

Ruthy looked toward the corner, too, and felt guilty. With the baby coming and Mr. Cooper's visit, she'd forgotten all about the little girl. Dorrie lay completely motionless, curled in a tight ball on Ruthy's bed, totally hidden under the covers.

"Dorrie?" Hannah called again "Honey?"

Dorrie didn't move.

"I'll get her." Ruthy walked over and pulled the cover back. Dorrie stayed where she was, eyes squinched tight. Ruthy patted the little girl's back. "Dorrie, come see the baby."

Eyes still shut, Dorrie shook her head. "No," she said.

"You're a big sister, now," Hannah said. "You're going to have someone to play with. Won't that be fun?"

More head shaking. Eyes still shut. "Not big. I'm little."

Ruthy laughed. "You don't have to be a big girl if you don't want to, but wouldn't you like to see the baby? Your mama misses you."

Dorrie opened her eyes and straightened her legs. "No. No baby."

Chuckling, Ruthy walked back to Hannah. "You heard her. She isn't coming."

"She'll come around," Hannah said. "She's hardly more than a baby, herself. It'll take awhile." Her eyes scanned the room. "I'd sure appreciate it if you'd redd things up a bit before Mrs. Cooper comes. Could you do that?"

"All right. What do you want me to do first?"

"Heat some water for starters. She'll need some. There's still some things me and her will have to do."

Harry had no sooner brought the water from the spring than Ruthy heard a wagon coming and a man's voice call, "Whoa, there."

Ruthy hurried to fill the kettle and poke up the fire. "They're here," she called over her shoulder. "Harry, tell the Coopers to come in."

Harry opened the door. "Ain't them," he said.

"Not them?" Ruthy echoed. "Who is it, then?"

"Don't know."

Puzzled, Ruthy went to look for herself.

It was Mr. Keeter, her friend from the wagon train. What in the world was he doing here?

Mr. Keeter gave a big gap-toothed smile and raised his hand in greeting. "Howdy, there, Miss Ruthy. I've come to take you home, if you're of a mind to go."

CHAPTER 39

Go or Stay?

Ruthy was so happy to see Mr. Keeter she clapped her hands. His arrival was a total surprise. This wasn't the most convenient time, but her friend's homely, familiar face brought a bit of comfort to a very hard day.

"I'm so glad to see you," Ruthy said. "What do you mean, take me back home? Did you find a place to settle? Are you going back to get your family? Do you have time to come in?"

"Whoa, there, Missy. Stop and catch your breath." Mr. Keeter said. He wrapped his reins around the brake lever and looked down at Ulysses. The dog stood just by the front wagon wheel, barking loudly. "I'll get down, soon as I know what this dog's going to do."

"He's friendly," Ruthy said. "Tie up and come in. I want to hear about everything. Have you heard where the Grogans are?"

"We'll have time to talk. First, though, I'd appreciate some water for my team."

"Of course. It's around by the barn. Harry will show you." Ruthy looked down at the boy standing by her side. She gave his shoulder a little push. "Mr. Keeter's my friend. From when I was coming from Tennessee to see you. Go help him."

Before Harry could move, Ulysses left the Keeter wagon and ran headlong toward the place where the road entered the clearing. His barks got even louder and his tail flapped wildly. It was Mr. and Mrs. Cooper, this time in their farm wagon. Without having to be told, they pulled around the house, heading toward the barn.

"Busy place," Mr. Keeter said.

"They're the Coopers," Ruthy said. "Our nearest neighbors. It's a long story. I'll explain in a bit."

Mrs. Cooper soon bustled in, carrying a bulging flour sack, talking as she came. "Hello, young lady. I'm Clara Cooper. You can call me Clara; no need to stand on ceremony. You must be Ruthy."

In a matter of seconds, Mrs. Cooper—Clara, Ruthy reminded herself—cleared one end of the table with a swish of her arm and began pulling things from her bag. "I brought supper," she went on. "A house is always at sixes and sevens when a baby comes. Nobody ever has time to cook, especially when it happens unexpected, like this."

Ruthy watched Mrs. Cooper lay out a big hunk of cheese, a pan of biscuits, half a ham, four big onions, and a pot of something that smelled like beans. Suddenly Ruthy remembered she hadn't eaten anything all day. Not since that one bite early this morning.

Next out of the sack came a large apron, big enough to wrap around Ruthy twice, but just right for the plump neighbor.

"Now then," Mrs. Cooper said, tying the apron behind her back. "How's our new mother?"

Ruthy wanted to say, "Don't ask me. You're the one who's supposed to know. " But Mrs. Cooper—Clara, Ruthy reminded herself again—looked as if she expected a reasonable answer, so Ruthy said, "The baby's awful little, but she's breathing. I haven't cleaned her up. At first there wasn't any water, then ..." Her voice trailed off in confusion as she thought of all that had happened since the baby was born.

"Well, let's go see how our new mother's coming along, shall we?" The older woman reached out one capable arm and swept Ruthy along to Hannah's bedside.

Feeling quite grownup at being included, Ruthy fetched and carried, watched, and listened. The midwife checked on Hannah's condition, explaining things to her young helper as she worked. By the time Hannah was dressed in a clean nightgown and the baby had been washed and swaddled in an extra blanket, it was dark outside and Ruthy's head whirled with all the new information.

Adding to her confusion, Mrs. Cooper chose that time to made a surprising offer. "Ruthy," she said, moving to clear the table, "you take to all this better than nearly any helper I've ever had. Ever thought about learning to be a granny woman? I've been hoping and hoping I'd find someone to pass all this on to. I tried to teach my own girls, but not a single one took me up on it."

"Oh, I couldn't, Mrs ... Clara. I'll be going home soon. In the spring, I hope. Or the summer, for sure." Ruthy said.

"Well, at least think about it. It's a good offer. You do have to go out in all kinds of weather, but if the baby and mother live, it's a special thing.

"And sometimes you even get paid. But then, again, sometimes you lose one or the other or both. The family certainly doesn't want to pay you for that. You'd have to learn how to take the bad with the good.

"Still," she said, winding up. "taken as a whole, it's a fine thing for a woman to do. I learned from my granny. She learned from her aunt. I'd teach you everything I know. It might be worth putting off your trip back home."

Not stopping for Ruthy to respond, and still talking, Clara—Ruthy remembered this time—finished clearing the table and laid out bowls and spoons. "Who was that other man at the barn?" she asked. Not waiting for an answer, she said, "I expect he'll stay for supper."

Finally, she drew a breath and stood back, surveying the food. Turning down one finger at a time, she counted, "Two of us," referring to herself and Mr. Cooper, "the stranger, you, Hannah, Harry, and Dorrie—that's seven. I guess we have enough. You can call the men to supper. I'll take Hannah's to her."

After supper and the dishes plus a final check on mother and baby, Mr. and Mrs. Cooper prepared to go home. Ruthy said they were welcome to stay if they didn't mind the floor.

"Thank you, but no. We have a hunter's moon," Mr. Cooper said. "so there's light enough to see our way. I still need to do the milking, and there's a batch of new hams in the smokehouse. That fire will need stoking."

"I'll ride over tomorrow to see how you're getting on," Clara said. She gave Ruthy a hug. "You did real good, Ruthy. I'd like to think my daughters would do as well under the circumstances, but I'm not sure they would. You're a brave girl. Hannah told me, awhile ago, she didn't think she'd have made it without you. Remember what I said. You have the makings of a granny woman."

"It was nice of Mrs. Cooper to say I was brave," Ruthy told Mr. Keeter later, in a moment of quiet by the fireplace after Harry and Dorrie were asleep. "But I wasn't brave at all. I was scared out of my wits. I didn't kill the wolf and if Hannah hadn't told me what to do, I would have been completely useless when the baby came." She stared at the fire.

"But you didn't stop trying," Mr. Keeter said. "That counts for a lot." He knocked his pipe out on the hearth and began to refill it. "I hate to push you, Miss Ruthy, when you've had such a hard day, but I ought to try to get away by mid-morning, tomorrow. Winter will soon be closing in and I hope to get home and back before the weather gets too bad.

He leaned forward, pulled a hot twig from the fire's edge, and lit his pipe. After a few puffs, he continued. "I didn't think I'd be able to take you when I went back, me being a lone man and you being a young lady all by yourself. But there's a widow woman driving her own wagon back, so as to be with her folks, just outside Knoxville. She plans to follow me for protection and such like. You could ride with her. Wouldn't cost you a penny. Said she'd be glad to have someone to talk with. So I come to see if you wanted to go."

Want to go? Of course she did. She'd dreamed about the day she could start home ever since she left.

Still, she hadn't thought she'd have a chance to go this soon. Childhood memories swirled through her head. Mama's cooking, Papa's rumbling voice when he said grace at the table, her own room and her own bed, petting Molly and sharing secrets with Josie. She had so much to tell everyone—about her trip and Cousin Nathan and Hannah and helping birth the new baby.

She longed to go home. Still ... Ruthy looked around the now-familiar cabin. Harry and Dorrie lay in their nest of quilts; Hannah and her little one were in the corner. If she left now, how would they manage until Nate came back? Who would milk and who would cook until Hannah got back on her feet?

Plus, she'd never be able to call the new baby by its name. She'd never hold her again and feel the sweet weight of the tiny head in the crook of her arm.

Just now, talking with Mr. Keeter, was the first time Ruthy had mentioned Clara's surprising offer out loud.

"I haven't told you" she said, "but Mrs. Cooper offered to teach me what she knows about bringing babies into the world. I'd have to stay here awhile longer but, if I did, she'd teach me everything she knows. She thinks I have a real feel for it." Ruthy reached for the iron poker and poked at the fire until sparks flew up the chimney.

"Well, now," Mr. Keeter said. He pointed the stem of his pipe at her. "That's a mighty big thing. But so is going back to your folks. Not an easy thing to get your mind around. Maybe you ought to sleep on it."

"I will," Ruthy said, grateful that her friend understood what a big decision she had to make.

Mr. Keeter cleaned his pipe one last time, stood, and headed toward the door. "I'll bed down in the barn." He paused. "Give me that milk bucket, there, and I'll tend to the cow before breakfast."

Ruthy handed him the bucket, paid a quick visit to the privy, banked the fire, and slipped into bed.

She tossed and turned through the long, dark hours, trying to decide what to do. The arguments for and against her decision rolled through her mind over and over and over again. Home right away or learning to birth babies? The comfort and safety of what she'd always known? Or hard work, far from home, learning to do things very few women could?

Ruthy sat up in bed, rubbed a kink out of her shoulder and flopped back onto the cornshuck mattress. A whippoorwill shouted its call nearby.

Another thing she had to think about was how she'd get home if she didn't go with Mr. Keeter. Who knew when the next ride would come along? Especially one that didn't cost anything.

Mama's letter said it looked like things were settling down, so they probably wouldn't mind if she came home earlier than they'd planned. What would Mama and Papa think if she didn't come back? She was their youngest, the only one left at home. Would they think she didn't care?

The whippoorwill called again. That was one loud-mouthed bird!

Ruthy yawned. If only she could shut her mind down,

maybe she could go to sleep. But the worrisome thoughts kept chasing each other around.

Supposing she stayed here in Missouri, where would she live? This cabin was already crowded and when the new baby started crawling . . .

What if Mrs. Cooper didn't turn out to be as nice as she seemed? What if she, Ruthy, found out being a granny woman was too hard?

Ruthy's sigh came all the way from her toes. If only she could talk to Mama and see what she thought.

Sometime before dawn, Ruthy finally fell asleep from sheer exhaustion, no nearer a decision than when she started.

Next morning, Ruthy staggered out of bed, dizzy from so little sleep. She hurried into her clothes, and checked on Hannah. The baby needed changing. Thankful for her experience with Feelie, she took care of that and laid her back by her mother.

She fried some of the ham left over from supper and stirred up a batch of cornpone. That, with honey and milk, would be a treat for everyone.

Breakfast over, she and Mr. Keeter lingered at the table. Harry went outside to play with Ulysses. Dorrie slid from her stool, came over to Ruthy's side, and held up her arms to be taken. She settled in Ruthy's lap, snuggled close, and stuck two fingers in her mouth. Ruthy's arms wrapped themselves around her small cousin as easily as if they had done it for years.

"Mr. Keeter," Ruthy said. One hand lifted from Dorrie's embrace and moved to trace mindless circles on the table-top. "If I decide to stay right now, do you think I'd be able to find another way home next spring or summer?"

"I 'spect so. They's people coming here from East Tennessee all the time. Stands to reason some of them would have to go back now and then."

"Would you go to see Mama and Papa and tell them why I didn't come home with you?"

"Why, sure," he said. "And you could send a letter too."

"You remember, don't you, when Kizzie was sick, back there on the trail, I said I wished I knew more about help-ing take care of sick people?"

Mr. Keeter nodded.

"Delivering babies isn't all I want to know about," Ruthy said, "but it's a place to start."

She paused. Even thinking about such a big step was scary. She felt lonely already.

"If I stay, do you think I could come see you and Mrs. Keeter sometimes?" Ruthy asked.

"Reckon you could. And we'd be glad to have you."

Ruthy chewed on her thumbnail. "I just don't know what to do. I miss home so much. But I'm not sure I can afford to go off right now and leave Hannah and the young ones ..." She laid her cheek on top of Dorrie's head. "If Cousin Nathan was here ..." She shook her head.

"Pardon an old man's advice, Miss Ruthy, but seems to me like you've already decided. Even if you don't know you have."

"I have?" Ruthy asked. If she had, it was news to her.

How could Mr. Keeter know what she thought when she didn't know herself?

"Yep. Think on what you just asked me. Could I talk to your folks. Could you come to visit us sometimes. Did I remember you've always wanted to know more about doctoring."

Ruthy thought about what her friend just said. She felt around, deep inside. As she did, something seemed to shift and settle. Her eyes filled with tears. "You're right. This is my chance, isn't it? And I really *am* needed here. At least for a little while."

Dorrie looked up, her attention caught by Ruthy's change of tone. "Ruthy cry?" she asked.

With a crooked smile, Ruthy shook her head and scrubbed the back of her hand across her eyes. "No, honey. I'm fine."

And she was.

She guessed she'd never stop missing Mama and Papa. But it wasn't as if she were leaving forever. She'd probably go back home next summer for certain. Between now and then, though, she could be a real help to her cousins. After all, they'd been willing to help her when she needed them, even when they didn't have much. This would pay them back a little bit. Plus, she—red-haired Ruth Ann Donohue—would make a start at learning how to take care of sick people. That would really be something.

And Clara said people might pay you real money for coming to birth a babe. Money was a good thing. Maybe, just maybe, Ruthy thought, she'd get that library and those bowls of candy all by herself, someday, whether the man she married was rich or not. At least she hoped she would.

Glossary

admonish—to give a scolding reminder

bile—a yellow digestive fluid that sometimes comes up in the throat when you feel like vomiting

chemise—a woman's one-piece undergarment, hanging from the shoulders; worn under a petticoat

clout—an early word for a cloth diaper

colicky—suffering from a pain in the stomach

county seat—the site of the county government

cranky—given to fretful fussiness

defendant—a person required to make answer, in court, for behavior

diapering cloth—a soft, absorbent cotton or linen fabric, usually white, woven with a distinctive pattern; so often used with babies that the usage finally came to be called, simply, "a diaper"

Dutch oven—a cast iron kettle with a tight cover used for baking over an open fire

elixir—a sweetened liquid usually containing alcohol that is used in medication

gew-gaw—a trinket or small ornament

granny woman—a name often used in the southern U.S., especially the Appalachians, for a midwife; sometimes extended to refer to a woman who knows how to use herbs as medicine

grippe—a viral infection, especially influenza

fowl—any bird; an adult hen

hunter's moon—a full moon that made the night bright enough to find one's way

infusion—a liquid made by steeping something like willow bark in water

juror—a member of a jury

jury—a group of persons sworn to give a verdict on a matter submitted to them, especially in a court of law

lean-to—a rough shed or shelter, often open on one side, having a roof with only one slope

M.G.—abbreviation frequently used in the 19th century for "Minister of the Gospel."

Midas—legendary king who had the ability to turn everything he touched to gold

nooning—a meal eaten at noon or a period at noon for eating or resting

Old Hundred—a song of several verses based upon Psalm 100 and sung to the tune known today as the *Doxology* or *Praise God from Whom All Blessings Flow*

outhouse—a small wooden building used as an outdoor toilet

pearl ash—a compound used before 1850 to make bread and cakes rise

peart—lively; in good spirits

poke bonnet—a woman's bonnet with a projecting brim at the front

privy—another word for outdoor toilet

raise Cain—to scold someone, especially loudly

redd—to make ready; to get ready

receipt—an early word for recipe

restriction—confinement within certain bounds

sal soda—a form of soda used to make cakes rise

sampler—a decorative piece of needlework typically containing letters and verses embroidered on it in various stitches as an example of skill

shift—a woman's loose-fitting slip or chemise

shun—to avoid deliberately

six bits—one bit is a unit of value. Six bits equals $\frac{6}{8}$ or $\frac{3}{4}$ of a dollar, or 75 cents.

sop—something, often a cloth, dipped in a liquid

square—An open, public space surrounded by buildings on all four sides, often with a courthouse in the middle

stock—shortened form of livestock, such as horses or cows

stoking—adding more fuel to a fire

teats—the protuberances (sticking out parts) on a cow's udder that you squeeze and/or pull to get milk

traction—the ability to catch hold of a surface without slipping

treadmill—an endless belt, often made of wood, walked on by animals in order to provide power

udder—a large organ hanging down just in front of a cow's hind legs that provides milk

verdict—the opinion or judgment of a jury

My Housewife Book
Collected by
Ruth Ann Donohue
(Begun in 1837)

I.
For Bad Indigestion

Crush a handful of charcoal and mix with a cup of milk. Drink all of it.

II.
Mrs. Patterson's Chess Pie

Boil for 15 min.—1 C. water, 1 T. vinegar, 1 T. cornmeal & 2 C. sugar (Brown or white or some of both)
Have the yolks of 9 eggs beaten well.
Add very carefully to the syrup, stirring constantly.
Add ¼ lb. butter, straight from the springhouse
Cook very slowly until butter is melted & eggs are about done.
Add 1 tsp. Vanilla
Put in unbaked pie shells. Bake slowly until pie is brown and stiff.
Makes 2 pies.

III.
Willow Bark Infusion for Fever

Cut the bark off of two or three young willow branches. Best if done in spring, then dried, but can be done at other times. Soak in cold water overnight. Heat slowly for a little less than a quarter hour. Strain and give to the patient slowly. (It tastes bitter and a dab of honey will help.)

IV.
For a Very High Fever

Put whole body in very cold water, or snow if you have it. Change the water to keep it cold until fever goes down.

V.
To Make Plum Leather

Wash and stem the plums. Start with a little bit of water and boil to a mush. Cool. Take out the seeds and as much of the peel as you can. Sweeten with honey. Boil again till thick. Pour onto clean boards and dry in the sun. Try to keep the flies and wasps away. When it's like leather, roll it up and store in a dry place. *Very Good*.

VI.
For a Head Cold

For a cold in the head, make a pot of hot chicken soup. Drape a warm cloth over the sufferer's head. Allow him to inhale the vapors. Then, serve a large portion, taken as hot as can be endured.

VII.
Mama's Cider Cake

For cider cake: One pound and a half of flour, half a pound of sugar, quarter of a pound of butter, half a pint of cider, one teaspoonful of pearl ash to make the batter rise; spice to taste. Bake in small loaves till it turns easily in the pans. About half an hour.

VII.
Proportions for a Pound Cake

One pound of flour, one pound of sugar, 10 eggs and ¾ of a pound of butter, the yellows of the eggs; butter and sugar to be beat well together. Add half a teaspoon full of cream of tartar to the dry flour, now work your flour in the other ingredients, then add the whites of the eggs well frothed, put the ¼ of a teaspoon full of sal soda in a tablespoon full of sweet milk, dissolved well, which add to the mass; beat the whole well together, flavor to your taste.

VIII.
Cure for Bite of a Mad Dog
Take immediately warm vinegar or tepid water and wash the wound clean, therewith; then dry it, then pour upon the wound a few drops of muriatic acid, because mineral acids destroy the poison of the saliva by which means the evil effect of the latter (that is the saliva) is neutralized. [*Author's note: This does not work but they didn't know that in 1837.*]

230

Mama's Recipe for Honey Cakes

Ingredients:

½ cup margarine or butter. (Mama used her own fresh
   butter.)
1 cup honey
½ tsp salt
1 egg, beaten
½ cup sour milk (If you have only sweet milk, add a tbsp.
   of vinegar to the milk.)
2 cups flour
1 tsp baking soda (Mama used "pearl ash.")
1 tsp cinnamon

Instructions:

Cream shortening. Add egg and honey; stir well. Sift
flour with baking soda, cinnamon and salt. Add the dry mixture alternately with the milk to the creamed mixture, stirring well after each addition. Bake in a well-greased 9X13
pan or in a muffin tin at 375 degrees until an inserted tooth-
pick comes out clean—about 50 minutes for a cake, 10-15
minutes for cupcakes. [Ruthy liked the small cupcakes
best.]

Make Ruthy's Sampler

You or someone in your family can make a cross-stitch sampler just like Ruthy's. It will come in a kit with everything you need. Motifs include Molly the Dog, the small church the Donohue's attended, Ruthy's journal, and several other items in Ruthy's life before she left home.

Contact Leslie's Craft Carousel by mail at 219 W. Jackson, Bolivar, MO 65613.

Selected References

Books

Child, Mrs. Lydia Maria Francis, *The American Frugal Housewife*, 12th ed. Boston: Carter, Hendee, and Co., 1833.

Fairbanks, Jonathan and Tuck, Clyde Edwin, *Past and Present of Greene County, Missouri*. Indianapolis, 1915.

Holcombe, R.I. (ed), *History of Greene County, Missouri*. St. Louis: Perkins and Horne, Publishers, 1883.

Josephson, Judith Pinkerton. *Growing up in Pioneer America: 1800-1890*. Minneapolis: Lerner Publications Company, 2003.

Laycock, George and Ellen, *How the Settlers Lived*, New York: David McKay Company, Inc., 1980.

Perry, John, *American Ferryboats*. New York: Wilfred Funk, Inc., 1957.

Peavy, Linda & Smith, Ursula, *Frontier Childhood*. Norman, OK: University of Oklahoma Press, Norman, OK, 1999.

Ristow, Walter, *American Maps and Mapmakers*. Detroit: Wayne State University Press, 1985.

233

Rubel, David, *The United States in the 19th Century*. New York: Scholastic, Agincourt Press, 1996.

Schimpky, David & Kalman, Bobbie, *Children's Clothing of the 1800's*. New York: Crabtree Publishing Company, 1995.

The Timechart History of America, Barnes & Noble, 2003.

Articles

1. Marshall, Ross, "River Crossings," *Overland Journal* (1991) 9:14.

Maps

1. "Travelers Guide to the United States," Philadelphia: Samuel Augustus Mitchell, 1837.

2. "Traveler's Guide Through the United States, A Map of Roads, Distances, Steam Boats & Canal Routes & etc." Philadelphia: J. H. Young, 1832.

Unpublished Material

1. Rountree, Joseph, "Diary of Joseph Rountree, 1782-1874," Springfield/Greene County Library, Springfield, MO.

About the Author

Louise A. Jackson grew up in a family of
storytellers. A fifth-generation Texan,
she presently lives in the Missouri
Ozarks and is the author of two previous
picture books. She likes to read, garden,
hike and travel, and collects antique
children's books about the American
West.

CPSIA information can be obtained
at www.ICGtesting.com
Printed in the USA
LVHW021041180520
655849LV00003B/462